THE
LEAVING

THE
LEAVING
Lynn Hall

Charles Scribner's Sons
New York

Copyright © 1980 Lynn Hall

Library of Congress Cataloging in Publication Data

Hall, Lynn.
The leaving.

SUMMARY: Roxanne's decision to leave her parents'
farm for a life in the city triggers other major
changes in her family.
[1. Family problems—Fiction.   2. Farm life—
Fiction]   I. Title.
PZ7.H1458Le   [Fic]   80-18636
ISBN 0-684-16716-6

5 7 9 11 13 15 17 19   F/F   20 18 16 14 12 10 8 6

Printed in the United States of America

THE
LEAVING

ONE

"Sooey, come pig, come pig."

Up from the barn toward the hog house a figure trudged, with buckets of grain stretching the arms down, apelike. It was a large figure in padded green coveralls, leather work gloves, an old blue stocking cap pulled down over ears and brow.

Roxanne's face, or what showed of it between cap and collar, was broad, somewhat big-nosed, skin not as fine-grained as she'd like but better than it had been a year or two ago. Her eyes were good clear hazel but short-lashed and rough-browed and didn't get noticed much. Her cheeks were chappy now with the cold drizzle blowing on them, and her lips felt rough.

"Come pig, here girls." Not that they needed calling. The four of them were standing just beyond the hog lot fence, grunting and shouldering one another away from the trough. Roxanne gave them one bucket, pouring its golden contents in a long, sibilant stream down the length of the trough, then she quickly gave the second bucket to the half-grown

1

young pigs at another trough, quickly so their mothers wouldn't bully them away from it.

Three more trips from grain bin to hog house, jam down the handle on the hydrant that had been filling the water tank, and the hogs were done for the evening. Roxanne always did the chores in the same sequence so that nothing would be forgotten, no hydrant left running, no eggs left ungathered to freeze and be wasted. She did the hogs first because they were her least favorite.

Then the cows. Climb up into the huge vaulted hay mow and throw twelve bales of hay out of the north door into the lot where the bull and eighteen stock cows waited, watching for their hay to come down, then crowding around the first bale so that the rest of the bales fell on their heads, on their ridged backs. Eight bales out the west door and down into the yearlings' lot where sixteen half-grown Herefords and one pinto gelding waited. Eight more bales out the east window to be carried, two at a time, across the frozen ruts of the hay field lane to where the newly weaned calves waited, bawling. Buckets of corn and oats to be carried to each group and water to be run into each tank.

As she heaved the last bales out the east door, trying not to let them break when they landed since they had to be carried to the weanlings, Roxanne pondered the area below, imagined it fenced in, a nice little feed lot connected to the hay field by a stretch of barbed wire so the calves could come up to

2

the barn for their hay and water, saving endless trips, carrying.

It would have been so easy for him to do, she thought resentfully. I told him and told him, and he never did it. Just put in a few good stout posts, string a little wire, and save all this work, all these years. Oh well, it's too late now. Too late for me. If he does the chores from now on maybe he'll see what I meant. Maybe he'll have a little more respect for my ideas when he's the one who has to haul all those bales.

Without conscious thought her body followed her mind through the work of carrying the bales over the frozen mud to the hay field, jabbing each bale in its middle with her knee until it buckled out of its twine, then throwing the loosened flakes of gray-green hay over the fence to the waiting calves. After each bale she looped the twine over the same rusted metal fence post where she'd been hanging it all fall. After all the work that went into cutting and baling that hay she could never quite bring herself to throw away the twine.

She returned to the barn through the yearlings' lot for a visit with Buck while the water trough finished filling. He was a good-natured little horse, a woolly, grimy red and white pinto with a multicolored mane that stood up in tufts where he rubbed it against the corner of the barn and wore it off. He had a rope halter about his head, and his lower lip hung slack, which gave him a deceptively stupid look. He had seemed quite large to Roxanne six years ago when her father brought him home from the sale barn and presented him to Roxanne for her twelfth birthday. Now he seemed short, but still as dear as ever. He walked beside her now, and her arm fell as comfortably over his withers as though they were old friends or lovers walking together in the comfort of habit.

"Maybe we'll go for a ride tomorrow, Buck. Would you like that? If the weather's nice. It'll be our last chance for a long time, old horse. My last day at home. But I'll come up for weekends sometimes, and we'll ride then, okay? Or at Christmas."

They stopped beside the hay bales, and Roxanne pushed aside the yearlings to break open the bales for them, to scatter the hay so the less aggressive calves got their share. She stood beside Buck and stroked down his wayward mane while he ate.

So hard, so hard to leave Buck and the calves. And the place.

She looked up and out, out the long lane that connected the farmstead with the highway beyond the cornfield. She saw herself and Buck and Norma, playing like children in the snow last winter. Norma had stayed over the night before so they could work on a class project and a snowstorm came in the night, closing all the county schools. The snow was deep but the day was warm and blindingly bright. They'd saddled Buck and tied an old inner tube to the saddle horn by a long rope, and spent the morning whooping and galloping up the long lane, one in the saddle and the other belly down on the inner tube.

Then they sat on the tube cross-legged to make a seat for Boots, who was following them barking frantically and trying to jump on. A wonderful day, and there'd be no more.

It was almost dark. Roxanne shook herself out of her sadness and filled her water and grain buckets for the chickens. It was raining in earnest now, rain that was just this side of sleet. She did the chickens quickly and went, head down, across the yard and into the house.

The kitchen was hot, bright, full of the sounds and smells of supper. Her father sat at the table, smoking, while her mother thwacked mashed potatoes into a bowl. Roxanne stood on the two steps leading up from the back door landing and kicked off her boots against the edge of the stair.

"Here," she said to her mother. From the breast pockets of the coveralls came three eggs, from the side pockets four more. Thora received them with a nod, a small satisfied grunt that Roxanne knew to mean, good, the hens aren't slacking off yet because of the cold.

She shed down to her corduroys, flannel shirt, and socks, then washed the barnyard fragrance off her hands and took her place at the table. She dished up silently and kept her eyes down toward her plate, but she felt a stillness between her parents that was somehow different from their usual lack of conversation, more deliberate. She looked up from her vegetables at Thora, then her father, risking eye contact, taking that chance. Both of them were eating with

5

such concentration they might have been alone, each of them alone in a separate house.

Thora was a big woman, handsome in a heavy way. A bulbous, man-sized nose dominated her face. Thick, iron-gray hair hung down her back in a single braid. Her mother's long hair used to embarrass Roxanne, especially when Thora didn't feel like braiding it and let it hang in a pony tail. Women her age didn't wear long hair. They were supposed to wear it short, or kinked a little, maybe. Like everyone else's mother.

Cletus Armstrong had long since lost the power to embarrass his daughter. He was what he was. Best to avoid him, ignore him when possible, fight him when necessary. He was tall, too, but spare, with thinning hair on top and pock-marked skin. Tonight he wore his sale barn clothes, frontier pants, Acme boots, denim jacket over a plaid shirt bright with all the requisite pearl buttons. The effect was dimmed by the rim of grayed underwear that showed at his neck.

"What was it doing out?" Thora said.

Roxanne looked away from her father, startled slightly. "Raining, pretty steady when I came in. Could freeze."

A few minutes passed in silence before Thora spoke again.

"You going to the game?"

"Yeah, I wanted to. It'll be my last chance. . . ."

Her voice faded. Thora nodded one slight nod. "You be careful how you drive. I don't want you driving fast. That rain could freeze and you not know it, and you'll pile yourself into a ditch somewhere, wreck the car."

"I won't," Roxanne snapped. She was an unusually careful driver and would have liked, just once, to be given credit for it.

They were almost finished eating when Cletus spoke. "Tomorrow night's horse sale night. I'll take Buck."

"What?" Roxanne shouted.

"No need to yell," Thora said placidly.

"Mom! Dad, you don't mean sell Buck? You can't do that. He's my horse."

Cletus shrugged and picked up his coffee mug. "You ain't going to be here. You'll be off in Des Moines living in some apartment. Horse won't do you any good there."

"But I'll be coming home for visits. Weekends and vacations. And when I get married and have kids I want to have Buck here for them to ride."

"He'll be long dead and gone by that time."

"No he won't, not necessarily. He's got a good ten years left in him. Mom—" She turned to Thora, pleading for support.

Thora shook her head and closed her mouth. I'm out of it, her face said.

Roxanne stared in disbelief at her father who was doing this to her, and at her mother who was letting him. She turned on Cletus.

"Well, he's my horse and I'm not selling him, and you can't make me."

Cletus took another long pull from his coffee mug.

"That ain't strictly true, girl. You think back to whose money bought that horse."

"Well, yours, of course, but you gave him to me for my birthday. If that doesn't make him my horse, I don't know what does."

"I gave him to you to use, and you've had the use of him all these years, and you've had free board and feed for him in my pasture, and my hay and oats and corn, and I've never begrudged you none of it."

Roxanne searched wildly for an argument so strong he wouldn't be able to fight it. But of course this wasn't the debating team, where the best logic won the contest. This was her father telling her what he was going to do, and logic was no match for paternal power. She fumed and she ached at losing Buck, and she ached for a mother who would have loved her enough to defend her against this outrage. She threw down her fork and pounded up the stairs to her room, shaking the house with her fury.

Roxanne's room was the only upstairs room that was in use, and it was selected because it was above the kitchen and was warmed in winter by a large floor register. When she came into the room she went through a maneuver she hadn't used for years, walking heavily across to the dresser, then crawling as silently as possible over the bed and stretching out on the braid rug with her head close to the floor register. All she could see through the grill of tan-painted metal was the top of the old wood stove in the kitchen below, a stove that was no longer used for cooking, only for heat. She turned her head to listen.

Now was the time. With her out of the room, Mom would lay into him, say, "You can't sell Roxanne's horse. It's not fair, and I'm not going to let you do it." She'd say, "Roxanne does more work around here than you do. She's more than earned that horse *and* his keep, and besides that, she's a good girl and I'm not going to see you make her unhappy."

"Now," Roxanne prayed.

She heard chairs scraping back from the table, dishes being scraped and stacked. Water running into the sink. The door opening, down to the landing where the coats and boots were.

Hurry up. Say something to him.

"See you later," Cletus said.

"Don't you get started drinking, now, after the sale. Those roads may be froze by that time." Thora's voice sounded heavy, as though she didn't care what he did but had to say her recitation anyway.

Too late. The chance was gone. At the sound of the back door closing Roxanne climbed to her feet and went to the window to watch with dull eyes as her father ran across the yard to the pickup. Boots cantered beside him, her tail wagging in its funny clockwise circles. Boots the traitor.

Beside the house, the lane made a circle. In the center of the circle was a small pump house and a very tall utility pole that held the yard light. Around the outside of the circle were house, machine shed, hog house, barn, chicken house. Roxanne could see, through the silver of rain under the yard light, the outline of Buck standing in the barn lot with the yearling calves, standing head down and ears lopping in the chilly rain.

She leaned against the corner of the dresser and smiled, remembering the night Buck came. It had been hot that night, six years ago in July. Her father had stood down there under the yard light and bellowed up at Roxanne's open window, "Wake up, Roxy, come and see your birthday present." She'd run down the stairs and outside, a stocky child in seersucker pajamas with the legs cut off short for summer. It was one-thirty in the morning, a magic time to be awakened and called outside. Her mother came, too, a bulky white shape with her hair blowing around her shoulders.

There was their stock truck with the tailgate down, and there came her father leading out a mammoth red and white spotted horse. Cletus made a bow as he handed her the lead rope. "Happy birthday, my girl. His name is Buckshot, and he's all yours."

"Really? Mine?"

"Really yours."

She reached up and gave her father a hug, awkwardly. She wasn't used to hugging him; she'd seldom had reason to. But now she had more than enough reason, not just a horse of her own, but proof that he loved her. Proof she could brag about to Norma, whose father openly adored her, and to the kids at school, to the whole world. My dad bought me a horse for my birthday. What a healing salve to rub into the hundreds of small hurts and neglects she had stored away against him.

For the next few years Buck was the center of Roxanne's life. He put her on an equal basis with Norma, whose family raised quarter horses and who had always had her own horse. Roxanne could ride with Norma when she wanted, or she could go off exploring alone, through her own large, rocky wooded pasture or down along the river or out on the gravel roads that wound and dipped through the valley.

Buck was her ticket to the inner circle of exhibitors each August at the Clayton County Fair. He had a stall in the 4-H horse barn, with his name and her name on a cardboard sign above the stall. Roxanne sat in the barn on a straw bale for two days each year, wearing her white and green 4-H tee shirt and feeling magnificently superior to the families who wandered down the barn's center aisle looking at the horses. Other 4-H kids were there, laughing, throwing things at each other, bathing their horses on the concrete platform at the end of the barn, and they were all part of the team, Roxanne included. Buck never won anything in his classes, but that wasn't important.

The last few years Buck was replaced to some degree by basketball. Their rides became fewer as Roxanne spent more and more time at the gym, practicing, or practicing at the rusted netless hoop on the front of the barn. But Buck still occupied a comfortable corner of her life. She knew he was out there in the pasture if she wanted him. He grew fat and tricky about being caught, but he was still her horse.

The clock beside her on the dresser said seven-thirty. The junior high game has been going for half an hour, and the varsity game would be starting by the time she got there. Sighing, Roxanne worked her feet into her shoes. These pants would be okay, the coveralls had kept them clean in the barn. She changed her farm shirt for a sweater, forgot deodorant and had to take the sweater off again, tried to comb her hair down so it wouldn't look funny, tried to squeeze a blackhead from her chin but only succeeded in making her whole chin red.

She clomped downstairs, determined not to speak to her mother.

"Have you got money?" Thora asked. She was drying the last of the supper dishes.

Roxanne nodded but kept her head turned away.

"Who are you playing tonight?"

A direct question. No way to avoid speaking, but she managed to mumble into her chest as she pulled on her jacket. "Valley of Elgin."

"You be careful of those roads, now."

"You told me that already."

"I'm telling you again." Thora's voice sharpened.

Roxanne let the door slam angrily, to make up for having been drawn into conversation. Boots romped as happily beside Roxanne as she had, earlier, beside Cletus, on the walk from back door to car.

12

"Oh, sure, you love everybody."

Boots dropped back a step, sensitive to Roxanne's anger. She was an ingratiating little border collie who was equally affectionate with people, cats, and cows. Before she got into the car Roxanne bent to reassure Boots. "I'm not mad at you, Bootsie. Just the rest of the world."

✝The Wadena high school building was one of the oldest in the county. It sat on a slight rise just outside a riverside village barely six blocks square, at the foot of a bluff whose crest was lighted by a giant cross. At night the hillside disappeared into the black sky, and only the cross was visible. On either side of school and village, the Volga River valley wound away out of sight. The Volga was a tiny river, deep enough for canoeing only in the spring, but the valley that followed it held beauty enough to grace the Mississippi, bottomland farms with sprawling brick buildings, hovered over by wooded, granite-creased bluffs. In the eight years that Roxanne had lived in the valley her first childish delight with the place deepened to a feeling that this was the one place in the world where Roxanne Armstrong truly fit.

Family roots? At first when she had become aware of the feeling, that was what she had assumed. Her mother had been born and raised on their farm, born in Roxanne's own room. Her father had grown up ten miles away on the other side of Wadena where his father still lived.

But that wasn't it, not really. It was something

13

more personal than grandparents. She'd hardly known her mother's parents and she didn't like her Grandpa Armstrong. And her own parents' childhoods meant nothing to her. They were as unreal as fiction. It was Roxanne who was important to Roxanne, and some strong but undefined part of her nature responded to the quietly impressive beauty of the Volga River valley, Clayton County, Iowa. Its beauty was of a subtle strength and needed to be lived with to be absorbed.

Tonight, as she drove to the school, she was glad for the darkness that hid the hills. She didn't want to have to see them. Too much was being taken away from her at once, home, the basketball team, and now Buck. And friends. Norma.

Well, it wasn't all gone yet. There was tonight and tomorrow. She parked the car and went inside, noticing as she went that the parking lot was half empty. Thanksgiving weekend, of course. Lots of people away for the weekend.

The concrete letters above the main door said, "Lincoln School, 1933." The hall was a giant U shape, classrooms on the outside, gym on the inside of the U. Opposite the front doors was a long glassed trophy cabinet. There weren't many trophies so they had to be spaced out along the shelves with drawings from the art department in-between. One of the trophies, second from the right, drew Roxanne's eyes as it always did, before she was through the inner doors. It was hers. Her team, last year, regional finalists in the state tournament, and her name was engraved on the front plate, second from the top. Above the trophy hung the team photograph, six girls in white and green satin uniforms, Roxanne's broad grinning face in the back row beside Norma's thin unsmiling one. The front-row girls kneeled in a semicircle around the ball, that good familiar ball. Mac, the coach, stood behind and above them all.

"Reminiscing, are you, Roxanne?"

It was Mr. Lister, her English and Social Studies teacher. He sat behind a card table that held a small gray cash box and a roll of cardboard tickets. He was young, blond, bearded, not quite tidy enough to look right with his Vandyke.

"Oh, yeah, I guess. You're not going to make me pay to get in, are you? The first game must be almost over."

"No, listen, former basketball stars don't have to pay to get into home games, especially on their last week in town. I hear you're leaving us. Going to seek your fortune in the big city, huh?"

"Something like that." She looked down and flushed. He could bring red to her face just by looking at her directly; he always had. It wasn't what he said, or even him, really, it was thinking about the dreams she had about him sometimes. Thinking by some horrible chance he might see the pictures in her head.

"Tell me about it. Unless you're in a hurry to get inside. The varsity game hasn't started yet."

"Oh, I'm just moving to Des Moines to get a job. Nothing exciting."

"It could be exciting, Roxanne. You'll get out of it what you put into it, you know. Why is it that you're going now? Why not last summer after you graduated?"

"I had to help at home, with the haying, and then I decided to stay till after we got the corn in, and we just finished that this last week. And besides, I figured in June there'd be an awful lot of competition for jobs, and I won't be able to afford to be without a job very long down there."

Mr. Lister nodded. "That's probably wise. Well, I wish you luck, Roxanne. That's a big bad city down there, you know." He rolled his eyes. "You're going to have to watch out for all those men. They go for these innocent country girls."

Roxanne laughed uncomfortably.

"Now listen," he went on, "here's my advice for you. If they corner you, cross your legs and light a cigarette. Got that?"

"Oh, Mr. Lister." She flushed again, and fought a smile, and he hooted after her as she turned away and went down the hall, dragging her thumbnail across the locker doors.

Rooms. Rooms. 102, Mrs. Graybeal; 104, Mr. Townsend; 106, Home Ec. Memories, not individual scenes so much as remembered emotions; the fear. Always the fear. Fear of being late, of coming in after the rest of the class was seated and quiet. Fear of not understanding something in the books or on the blackboard and being ridiculed because everyone else knew what it was all about. But those were mostly the elementary school fears that somehow followed Roxanne to high school, where they lay beneath the surface of newer anxieties, like being certain there was never a red spot on the back of her skirt, and camouflaging the fact that no boy, ever, singled her out for attention. And through it all was woven a continual threat. Tests. Weekly tests, semester tests, surprise quizzes, when even the facts she had firmly memorized wafted away in the pressure of *having* to know it right now.

Funny, she thought as she peered into one empty classroom after another, funny to be beyond it all now, to be here in the building, still the same Roxanne Armstrong, and to be impervious to the power of this place. She had survived it. Not graduated at the top of her class or even in the top third, but graduated.

Her stomach coiled at the thought of what she was going to have to do now. Move to a strange city where she knew no one. Apply for jobs. *Get* a job and learn to do it before she was fired for being inept and stupid. Compared to what lay ahead of her, in terrifyingly few days, this school grew suddenly warm and reassuring around Roxanne. At least here she'd had her place. She was Roxanne, Roxy, C student, a farm kid like most of her classmates, a guard on the basketball team, glee club member, best friend of Norma Zimmerman, who was talented. Everyone knew Roxy. But then in a hundred-student high school, everyone knew everyone. In a bigger school Roxanne Armstrong would never have come to the surface, and no one knew that better than Roxanne.

And now she was going to have to tackle Des Moines.

Don't think about that tonight.

Inside the gym the atmosphere in Roxanne's head changed almost instantly. In here were the sounds and smells of basketball; thump-thump of dribbled ball, staccato trills of referee's whistle, the ruffling rustling of the hundred or so people in the bleachers. Ah, this was home.

She slid along the second-row bleachers to a seat just behind Mac and the non-playing team members. The varsity game was just a few minutes along. On the high-gloss golden floor, twelve tall girls moved in a tense dance, six on either side of the center line in the six-player, split-court game peculiar to Iowa, intended to be less tiring than the full-court game the boys played but serving only to frustrate the players who were held away from the action by the center line. Roxanne could feel it from where she sat, the bursting energy, the need to move and keep moving and get in there where the action was. Her feet shifted against the seat ahead of her, her fingers stretched out around that cowhide sphere, felt the life in the ball.

Mac turned and smiled up at her and gave her foot a squeeze, then turned back to his players. Looking down on his shiny, gray-fringed head, his round face and too-small glasses, Roxanne felt her throat ache and swell. This was the father she hated to leave. She'd left him already, at graduation, but this second leaving was going to hurt just as much.

Roxanne propped her legs up, elbows on knees, chin in palms, and let her mind wander away. It wasn't the games she remembered with pleasure; for her the games had always been marred a bit by knowing everyone was watching her. By knowing that her parents were not watching her. By the fact that her team lost more often than they won. No, the good memories were the practice sessions when she and Norma and Alene and the others were alone out there, and the feelings were good. They all liked each other, and most of all they liked Mac. It was fun, running through the practice formations, leaping toward the basket and hearing from Mac either, "Good one," or "Oops," which was his strongest form of correction. Laughing at nothing, feeling that she was as much a part of the group, as important a part of the group, as anyone.

The good memories were sitting around in Mac's backyard on summer afternoons and being talked into a game of jacks by one of his younger children, being pressed to stay for supper, hamburgers on the grill. Being balanced in an oddly comfortable way between having sexy dreams about Mac and knowing, somehow, that neither he nor Mrs. Mac would be upset if they knew.

The good memories were the out-of-town games. Oh, they were the best of all of Roxanne's memories. There was an excitement about boarding that mus-

19

tard-colored school bus with the rest of the team and Mac and his family and the cheerleaders, an excitement out of proportion to the actual experience. Driving forty miles to a school much like her own, playing a game of ball, listening to Mac say, "You girls played a good, honest game and I'm just as proud of you as if we'd won," driving home again to cold cars waiting in the school parking lot. It was not so much what happened on those trips that generated the excitement, it was what might possibly happen. She could be out there playing away, in front of a strange audience, and somewhere among those faces in the bleachers, there might be a boy who could not take his eyes off Roxanne Armstrong. He would be her kind of boy, not one of the handsome ones, nor one of the top students, but valuable in his own way, as she felt sure she must be valuable in her way if only she knew what it was.

Someone of her own. Oh, what an ache there was in that wish.

It never happened, of course, but as long as there were out-of-town games the possibility existed.

The horn signaled the end of the first quarter and brought Roxanne's head up from her hands. Norma was climbing up beside her.

"How you doing?" Roxanne said.

Norma shrugged and sent a telling glance at the scoreboard. She was a long, narrow girl with a long, narrow, somber face warmed by gentle brown eyes. Now, as always during a game, her skin bore a sheen

20

of perspiration and her hands trembled. She had always seemed older than Roxanne, even when they were children, although she was in fact a year younger.

"Oh well," Roxanne said, "we've got plenty of time to catch them. It's just the first quarter."

Norma shrugged as though she didn't really believe that but it didn't matter. Roxanne knew better. Everything Norma did she did with intensity, and it was never good enough for her, not her ball playing or her drawing, which was surely good enough to assure her a future in commercial art, and in which her parents had already invested four hundred dollars for a correspondence course in Learning Art At Home. Norma's talent was a thing of pride for her parents, and for Roxanne in her position as best friend, but it was an almost crushing burden of responsibility to Norma.

"Listen," Norma said, "I think Alene's coming home for the weekend. Why don't the three of us go out and do something tomorrow night? Do you want to? It can be your going-away party."

"Good. Sure. Let's go for supper, shall we? I can probably get the car. I'll pick you up."

The horn sounded and Mac slapped Norma's ankle, sending her out again with the rest of them. Across the floor and up on the stage was a long table where the officials sat, and the sportscaster from the local radio station. Behind them stood a small bleachers for the visiting team's cheering section. It was almost empty. Roxanne didn't bother to scan it for faces of interesting boys. Even if He did show up now, it would be too late.

She turned and looked instead at the home team bleachers, the big ones that ran the full length of the gym behind her. The crowd was thin and scattered tonight, leaving yards of bare golden wood at either end of the gym. Small boys in flopping galoshes played chasing games around and under the bleachers, leaving gray, watery bootprints on the shiny wood. There was a scattering of older faces, round plain faces above flannel shirts and overalls and bright knit suits, faces of the players' families, of town people and farm people for whom the Friday night ball games were a pleasant, if not quite exciting, way to spend Friday nights, away from the television set and with their neighbors.

Between the whooping children and the game-watching middle-agers was the balance of the audience, teenagers who hardly bothered to watch the players at all in their absorption with one another, and the teachers who, in many cases, could hardly be told from the students. Few were past thirty. It was a small school system and its low pay scale drew the young teachers fresh from college who lacked the experience to get better-paying jobs in larger towns. The youth of the teachers, and the feeling among them that they were here only temporarily, engendered an informality between teachers and students that bordered on equality, at least in the high school.

So different from her old elementary school in Waterloo, Roxanne mused. So much smaller and kinder and safer. It occurred to her that she might never again be here in this gym, in this school. In a perverse way the pain of that thought propelled her into leaving; she did not want to wait till the game was over. She just wanted to get out of the gym and get it over with.

Outside, the rain had turned to frozen pebbly stuff on the sidewalk, on the cars. She had to hack and scrape a hole in the windshield ice, then sit huddled over the wheel waiting for the defroster to begin making itself felt on the inner surface of the glass. Now that she was outside, she wished herself back in the warm, friendly gym again, back kidding around with Mr. Lister, or sitting with Norma's mom and dad and watching the movement of the game, back and forth from one court to the other, the scrambles under the net, the ballet of the jump-offs, the orderly lineups for free throws.

But it would look silly to go back in now. She thought about driving to Elkader or West Union, see if there was anybody she knew at the drive-in or the bowling alley or skating rink. But the roads were too icy. And besides, she realized dully, there wouldn't be any of her friends there. They were all gone. Long gone. Some to college, some to jobs in cities where the jobs were, a few into marriages that seemed to remove them from sight as effectively as a geographical move.

I'm the only dinosaur left, she thought, almost smiling. And I'm about to disappear, too. Yes. Dis-

23

appear. To a place she'd never even seen, that she had chosen as her testing ground because it was the state capital, the biggest city in Iowa, the ultimate arena. Survival there would be proof enough of Roxanne Armstrong's guts, even for Roxanne Armstrong.

Because she could think of nothing else to do, she shifted and eased the car out onto the ice-coated drive. Even at minimum speed the car had almost no turning power and she had to back-and-forth several times in slow motion to get safely out of her parking place. As she crept along the village street and out onto the blacktop she imagined that she was in the school bus tonight, with the rest of the team and Mac and they were going home from an out-of-town game when the bus went into the ditch. No one badly hurt but they were stranded overnight in some warm, secluded place, and conveniently the rest of the team disintegrated from the dream and left her and Mac, and the only place for them to sleep was together on a big bed, no, a narrow bed so they'd have to lie close together, with his arm around her and his face close to hers.

Roxanne was so light-headed from her imagining that she let the car gather speed, and had to brake a bit, causing the car to skid frighteningly on a curve. She grew rigid, but managed to get the car balanced and centered again, and slowed to a safe speed. Thank God nobody was coming, she breathed. What if I'd had a bad accident?

Then I wouldn't have to go to Des Moines.

She smiled at herself but the smile faded as she

24

realized how close she was to meaning it, to preferring that her life end right now, while she was still here and happy, before the next chapter started.

That's stupid, Armstrong.

You don't have to go, you know. You could stay home and help on the farm till you got married. Some girls do.

Oh sure. Look at the girls who do that. Look at Lucille Koehn. She stayed home. She's a borderline idiot and couldn't have gotten a job if she'd tried. And that Evelyn What's-her-name, she was so ugly, and so shy, everyone knew she stayed home after she graduated because she was just too scared to do anything else. Well, they're not going to say that about me.

She eased off the highway into the safe roughness of her home lane. When she parked the car and got out she found that her legs were trembling with residual fear and the ache was still in her chest from the squeezing of her heart.

Her mother was watching the ten o'clock news in the living room.

"Were the roads bad?" Thora asked, not looking up.

Roxanne thought, I nearly got killed tonight and she doesn't even turn off the TV when I come in. I wonder if she'd care if I'd got killed? I wonder if my funeral would have been too much of a nuisance for her to go to.

Thora looked up. "Were the roads bad?"

"Yeah," Roxanne muttered. She was suddenly so

full of anger she could hardly speak to her mother, and yet the anger seemed to come for no specific reason. It was just there. She needed to yell, and there was nothing to yell about.

Thora's eyes were back on the television screen. "Denny said freezing rain tonight, maybe turning to snow by morning. He said partly cloudy and colder by Sunday. I hope our roads aren't bad Sunday."

"Sure you do. You might have to keep me around a few more days if we got snowed in. You might have me underfoot a while longer, Mother. Well I promise you this, I'm leaving Sunday if I have to hitchhike to Des Moines, so you can rest easy on that point."

Thora turned and stared, her mouth loose. "Roxanne!"

"Oh I know, Mother. I know just exactly how important I am to you. You sit there and let him say he's going to take my horse away from me and sell him. You could have said something. You could have stuck up for me, but you just sat there. That tells me just exactly what you think of me."

Before Thora could gather her breath Roxanne went on. "And do you know something else? All this time, the whole three years that I played on that varsity basketball team, when I was one of the best players on that team, did you ever once come to watch me play? You or Dad, either one?"

"He's always worked Friday nights at the sale barn," Thora said in an uncharacteristically weak voice.

"But not you. You could have ridden into town

with him when he went to the sale barn, or you could have ridden in with me, or with Norma's folks. Norma's folks never missed one home game, did you know that? The whole town sees Norma's mom and dad sitting up there in the bleachers watching their daughter, being proud of her, and it's not fair. I'm as good a player as Norma. Better. And there was never anyone there watching me. How do you suppose that made me feel? And if my own parents don't love me, what in the hell are the chances that anyone else in this crumby world is ever going to?"

Roxanne heard her own words and fled from them, fled upstairs to the shelter of her room. She hadn't even known she was thinking those things, and now the words were echoing around down there in the living room.

She stopped in the doorway to her room and listened. Denny was back on again, his buoyant, boyish voice giving the weather wrap-up at the end of the news.

That'll take her mind off of me, Roxanne thought. The anger was gone out of her now, but she was too strung up to go to bed. She turned on the radio and lay down, clothed, to listen to the last few minutes of the ball game.

Valley of Elgin won.

TWO

Thora's thoughts were not focused; her mind jumped in many directions as she scooped the mashed potatoes from pan to serving dish—toward Clete, who sat silently at the table behind her, waiting for the food to be served so he could eat and escape; toward Roxanne out in the rainy dark, coming in now from finishing chores; on the three pans on the stove and what had yet to be put on the table, butter and sugar and salt shaker.

As Roxanne came in and began kicking off her boots, Thora's attention centered on the girl. Good, solid Roxanne. Good, quiet Roxanne who never questioned the fact that she was out throwing hay bales and carrying water buckets while her father sat here waiting for his supper. Roxanne, who was as eager to be gone from Thora as Cletus was. Why?

The anguish of the question made not the slightest ripple in Thora Armstrong's expression.

"Here," her daughter said, handing her eggs from the pockets of her coveralls. Dear hands, as big and square and red as Thora's own hands, with the same blunt, broad nails on fingers that held the eggs with

28

gentle confidence. Thora wanted to touch those hands, to hold onto them and keep Roxanne here on the farm with her, where the girl belonged. She didn't trust her voice just then, so she merely made a small wordless sound, to show satisfaction with the egg count, and turned away to put the eggs in the refrigerator.

She dished up and sat down with the others, and began passing. Clete was tense. She could hear it in the way he used his silverware, clacking it against the plate. Something was building in him. He was about to say something and Thora didn't want to hear the words that she could almost visibly see rising in the man.

She turned to Roxanne. "What's it doing out there?" The girl jumped. She feels the tension, too, Thora thought.

"Raining, pretty steady when I came in. Could freeze."

Thora turned back to her food to hide her thoughts. Freezing rain, on a night when both of them were going out in it, driving to town, coming home late. Freezing rain, the thing Thora dreaded most deeply with every approaching winter. Black highways silvered with ice, cars that couldn't turn or stop, crashing into each other, faces ripped through windshields' broken glass, crushed bodies—no. She fought the pictures, squeezed them out of her mind.

"You going to the game?" she asked. Maybe by some miracle Roxanne would decide to stay home tonight, her almost-last night at home.

"Yeah, I wanted to. It'll be my last chance—"

Thora nodded. Of course that would be Roxanne's choice. An almost imperceptible edge of hurt showed through in her voice. "You be careful how you drive. I don't want you driving fast. That rain could freeze and you not know it, and you'll pile yourself into a ditch somewhere, wreck the car."

"I won't," Roxanne snapped.

Thora withdrew. Her own last words had sounded as though she were more concerned about the car than about Roxanne. Although she made no audible sound, a deep inward sigh went through her. Eighteen years of being Roxanne's mother and she still hadn't learned how to say things so they came out sounding the way she meant them.

Suddenly Clete said, "Tomorrow night's horse sale night. I'll take Buck."

Thora stiffened. So that was it, then. He was planning to sell Buck. Knowledge broke over Thora. Sell Buck and pocket the money, and make his move. It was coming. It was coming now. He was going to do it, and he didn't have any money of his own to do it with, so he was going to sell Buck.

She was aware that Roxanne was pleading with her for support, but she had no words, not even wrong ones. She could only shake her head. Their voices battered back and forth across her, Cletus who had the power, and Roxanne who had the right. Thora hurt for Roxanne's hurting, but she couldn't lean in Roxanne's direction. She could see what Roxanne could not see; Cletus had his need, too, and it was bigger than hanging onto a pet horse. Roxanne was about to move away permanently and she'd be leaving the horse anyway. It had to go Cletus's way, and it would.

Roxanne slammed out of the room and pounded up the stairs. Thora heard her moving softly across the room, approaching the floor register. Wordlessly she got up and began clearing the table. She had an almost overwhelming urge to say something to Clete, like "I know why you're selling Buck, and I'm not going to stop you because I want you to do what you're going to do. I want it just as much as you do, so don't get the idea you're putting one over on me. You couldn't fool me, you son-of-a-bitch, not the best day you ever lived."

✦She poured soap into the sink and turned on the hot water full blast, till it bit her wrists. Behind her she heard him get up, stretch, go for his jacket. Go on, she willed, get out of my house.

"See you later," he said.

In an effort to sound as though she cared as much about his safety as she had, earlier, about Roxanne's, Thora said, "Don't you get started drinking now, after the sale. Those roads may be froze by that time."

He grunted and left, and after a while, when the dishes were almost done, Roxanne left, too.

It was odd, Thora mused, how a person could feel bad about being left behind even when she didn't truly want to go. Going with Clete to the Friday night cattle auction was the last way in the world she'd have chosen to spend this evening. And she had long

31

since given up the hope that Roxanne would say, Hey, Mom, why don't you come along and watch the game with me? Still—

She poured herself another cup of coffee and turned on the kitchen radio, then settled herself in her mother's old caneback rocker in the corner of the kitchen. She rested her feet on the stepstool under the telephone and set her coffee cup on the counter where she could reach it.

It wasn't time yet for the varsity game to start, and the junior high game wasn't broadcast. The radio was still on Friday Night Polka Party.

I don't even know why I'm listening tonight, she thought, with Roxanne not even on the team any more. Habit, I guess.

So many habits. Her whole life was habits. And they were about to be blown away.

Thora Braun was twenty when she met Clete Armstrong. She was a rangy young woman, loosely strung together, with soft brown hair crimped by Toni Home Permanents, broad shoulders and hips beneath her cotton housedresses, sturdy ankles in white anklets. Her nose was substantial then, but it hadn't yet assumed the dominating proportions that were to come later.

In the house, in the presence of her parents, Thora was so quiet as to be nearly mute. Her presence was an apology for itself. But outside, away from them, she talked almost continually to whatever animals she was near. The cattle were her favorites, and the team of work horses with which her father plowed and cultivated because of the scarcity of fuel to run the old Deere tractor. She enjoyed the sheep, too, the half dozen of them whose job it was to keep the yard and orchard mowed. But it was the chickens who consumed the largest part of Thora's time. She kept a clean, healthy flock and the egg money most weeks was enough to cover whatever groceries needed to be bought.

Since the beginning of the war more and more of the farm work attached itself to Thora as her older brothers, one by one, walked through the jaws of the recruiting office and came back in the form of telegrams of regret. With each death Gunnar and Elvira Braun seemed to grow smaller and more brittle, until in the end what had been a large, strong, young family was just a bitter old man, an equally bitter old woman, and a daughter who felt, rightly or wrongly, that they resented her for being female and therefore being the survivor, when what they needed to run the farm was sons.

Obviously Thora could not give Al, Tom, and Gunnar, Jr. back to her parents, but it was within her power to give them one son, and future grandsons, and she was determined to do it. She was aware that she had qualities that made her valuable on the marriage market. She was sole heir to a good farm, she was nice-enough looking, she was strong and healthy and hardworking. In a community like Wadena she was ideal wife material. The only problem was that almost all of the young men who would have been potential husbands and sons-in-law were in foxholes in Germany.

Still, she was determined to find one for herself, for her parents. For the farm. She'd had her dreams, of course, of what her husband would be like. Big, gentle, easygoing, the kind of man who would enjoy the beauty of the farm along with her. The kind of man who loved children and animals and who would not be afraid to admire flowers. She always envisioned him with black hair and blue eyes and fine-grained skin and rather full, soft lips, and a blue-plaid flannel shirt.

When Clete Armstrong jumped down from the tailgate of a stock truck and walked up her lane one August afternoon in the summer of her twentieth year, Thora saw in him none of the characteristics of her dream husband. Tall, yes, but narrow-tall, with hair cut so short it hardly had any color except what was reflected from his skin. His features were thin and his voice had a twang that might have been Missouri or Arkansas or just back-roads Iowa. But he did have one characteristic that outweighed the absence of all the others. He existed. And as he stood there at the edge of the vegetable garden where Thora was hoeing, as he looked down at her and asked if by any chance they could use a hired man, his eyes seemed to glow upon her as though she were the girl of his dreams, just discovered.

She reasoned that if she couldn't marry the man of her dreams, and that seemed impossible given the field she had to choose from, the next best thing would be to marry a man to whom she was the dreamed-of desire.

By the time the wedding took place seven weeks later, the disappointments were already beginning. Her parents did not greet her gift of a son with the joy Thora expected, nor even with a noticeable show of relief that there would be help with the farm work in time for the fall harvesting. The two silent, gray-haired figures remained silent, dull-eyed. They were polite enough to Clete but they treated him as a visitor. And the hostility that had come to be their habitual attitude toward Thora remained, and perhaps deepened.

For the first time since her brothers had begun dying, Thora felt some righteous anger of her own. For them, for those two old crabs who barely spoke to her at meals, she had thrown away what chance there might have been for finding her smiling black-haired man and had handcuffed herself to this Cletus Armstrong person for the rest of her life. And they showed not the slightest sign of gratitude, or even of recognition of her sacrifice.

Perhaps not total sacrifice, she told herself during those autumn days. Clete was pleasant enough and kind enough, but there were holes in her happiness in that direction, too. He seemed—distant. He seemed to be focused somewhere else most of the time that they were together, as though they were so familiar with each other that there was no need to concentrate on her. Memories from the war, she told herself. After all, he'd only been discharged a few months, and his head must be filled with terrible things from over there. So she was determined to be patient about that. Still, it was a letdown to realize that she had read him wrong at that first meeting, that apparently the love at first sight had been imaginary.

There was something that bothered her even more than their mutual lack of love. Love, after all, might very well grow over the years as they raised their family and created a home together here on the farm. What was worse than lack of love was lack of balance between them. Thora was smarter than he was. There was no way around that fact. She made little jokes sometimes in the privacy of their bedroom, and he looked at her as though he wasn't quite sure how she meant them. His mind seemed always a step or two behind hers. It was usually Thora or her father who directed Clete's time, who told him this would be a good day to be sure the corn picker was oiled and ready to go, or this would be a good day to move the weaning-age calves into the hay field.

The more she led, the more he dropped back and let her lead, and the more he dropped back the more she took over. Somebody had to, and his withdrawal created a vacuum into which Thora, whose strength had until now been overshadowed by brothers and parents, was pulled not entirely against her will. By mid-winter the pattern between them was set.

In winter the farm work was light, no more than just the everyday chores. Gunnar took care of the morning and evening milking, which was the most time-consuming of the chores. Clete had made a tentative offer, once, to do the milking. Gunnar ignored the offer and it wasn't repeated. Thora did the rest of it, the feeding and watering and egg-gathering just as she had before the marriage, but now she was doing it as much to get out of the house as for any other reason. She could have handed it over to Clete, but then she would have been trapped inside with her mother, who spent much of her time listening to the radio and staring at her African violets.

Clete developed a unique ability that winter, the ability to disappear. With no foot-stomping of shoes into boots, no announcements of errands in town or notices when to expect him back, he would simply not be there. Later he would appear from the direction of the basement or one of the unused bedrooms upstairs, or from a strange car or truck slowing to let him out at the mailbox. Thora didn't ask where he'd been, and he didn't volunteer information.

It will be better in the spring, Thora thought. But it wasn't. It was worse, much worse. One evening in March Clete announced that he had been to Waterloo, that he had a job in the John Deere plant starting Monday, that Thora should start packing their things.

She tried to talk him out of it, to impress upon him what the farm meant to her, and what his help, and hers, meant to the farm, *especially* in spring when there were solid days of cultivating and planting that must be done besides the daily chores and the calving and lambing. But he had never formed the habit

37

of hearing her and Thora, who had no love for him and knew he had none for her, was without a powerful lever. He had decided, and she had no choice but to start the packing.

As she walked around the farm those last few days, breaking inside herself, she probed the possibility of simply staying here, letting him go live in Waterloo. But there was no precedent in her experience for that sort of split marriage. You married a man and you lived with him. If he were terribly cruel or a drunkard or got mixed up with another woman it was possible to leave him, but even then a good share of the guilt would land on you, and on your family. And Clete had made none of the giant errors that would have allowed her this escape route. So in private Thora patted the barn good-bye and spoke to the chickens, the milk cows, the lamb-heavy ewes, and told them she'd be back.

Several generations of livestock came and went before Thora and Cletus Armstrong came back to the farm. Twenty-two years. Twenty-two years of living at Lot 3212 of the HiWay Mobile Home Park, of sitting in her aluminum coffin with nothing to do but watch television and, later, see to the needs of her daughter. Clete forbade her to get a job, forbade the buying of a second car, so that she was virtually imprisoned at home. Public transportation in this small industrial city was sketchy at best, and came nowhere near the HiWay Mobile Home Park.

For eleven years Thora gritted her teeth and took it, took the grinding boredom and the panicky feeling that her youth, the best part of her life, was being drained away and she could do nothing to stop it. She was just working up to doing something about it, divorcing Cletus and getting her life back into her own hands in whatever way she could, when the pregnancy she had longed for in the early years became fact, and Roxanne was there, needing a father. Everyone knew a child needed a father.

Thora cried a great deal during the pregnancy and just after. It was the only time in her life that she cried about anything, and what she was crying about then was too silly to tell anyone. A black-haired, blue-eyed, smiling man in a blue-plaid flannel shirt who was never going to be this baby's father.

At first it was hard for Thora to be anything more than just a technical good mother, to keep the baby clean and fed and quiet. But as Roxanne became a person, able to converse with Thora, the two of them grew close. Clete was almost never at home when Roxanne was awake. His shift at the factory led directly into his shift at the pinball machines at one of the bars near Deere's. There were no other preschool children at HiWay then, and Thora had no close friends with small children, no close friends at all for that matter.

At first it was awkward for Thora to respond to the child's desire to be cuddled. Thora had no memories of soft laps and warm arms from her own childhood, nor had there been anyone in her adult life to condition her to spontaneous giving. Only when Roxanne fell and came crying with scraped elbows or knees could Thora forget her own awkwardness and open her arms. "Summer knees disease," she would say as she painted the raw kneecap with Mercurochrome, then blew on it to make the sting go away.

One day when Roxanne was four and in a particularly attention-demanding mood, Thora grew irritated at her and shooed her away. Several minutes later the child was back, rubbing her eyes with a false sort of sniffing sound, and saying, "Summer knees disease, Mommy." On her knee was a bright red wound made of crayon.

After that Thora made the small effort to push herself past the initial awkwardness of touching and cuddling, and the closeness between them intensified. As long as Roxanne was the focus, Thora could push the rest of her life into the background— the trailer and Clete and the town and the boredom. Roxanne was almost enough.

And if Roxanne were not sired by the smiling black-haired man who should have been Thora's husband, at least she appeared not to be Clete Armstrong's daughter either. The sturdy, broad-shouldered child was all Thora. Everyone said so, and Thora began to see Roxanne as herself reborn, a second chance for all the good things that life was apparently going to withhold from Thora Braun Armstrong.

But then came school, and Thora was no longer the center and substance of Roxanne's days. Roxanne began bringing other little girls home with her to play after school, and Thora fought waves of frightening, disgusting jealousy. Who ever heard of a mother not wanting her child to have friends? Thora withdrew, hoping Roxanne would notice and come after her asking for hugs, showing faked summer knees disease. But Roxanne's world was opening. It was full of alphabets and games and new people her own age to explore for the first time in her life, and she didn't notice her mother's new quietness.

Clete was a nearly invisible member of the family during those years. He seldom came home before Thora was asleep, and she developed the habit of sleeping, or pretending to, until after he was gone in the morning. On weekends he was usually off with friends from the plant, friends Thora never met. They spent the long weekend days at the Sports Club on the river, where they shot on the rifle range and drank beer.

The salary Clete earned would have been enough —more than enough—to give them what Thora wanted most, a house in the country, and when they discussed it Clete always agreed that yes, it would be nice to have a house, a dog, a pony for Roxanne, and yes, he'd start putting away a little toward the down payment. But somehow the down payment money always melted away into the cash register at the bar where Clete and his friends spent their evenings, or into the expensive rifles that began to accumulate in the corners of the trailer, and Thora began to understand that it was never going to happen. Clete was simply too comfortable with the life he had, to make any effort to change it.

Then, when Roxanne was ten, Elvira Braun developed cancer of the throat. From the farm where she was installed in the bedroom off the living room, unable to speak, she wrote notes of terrified pleading not to be sent to a nursing home.

Thora laid it out to Clete in flat tones. "I'm going back. I gave twenty-two years of my life to you and this place, and that's enough. I belong on the farm. It's where I've always belonged. They need me there very badly now, and I'm going. You can come, or not. Suit yourself."

She was surprised, and he was, too, when Clete turned in his resignation at Deere's and staked a For Sale sign into the grass in front of the trailer.

"You're not taking my daughter away from me," he said. "Roxanne needs her daddy, and as long as she needs me I'm going to be there."

It was his first expression of fatherly love since the early days after Roxanne's birth; it was also the last, except for the unexplained appearance, two years later, of the red and white pinto pony.

Early in the second half of the ball game Thora turned off the radio and the kitchen light, and moved to the dark living room. She didn't want to know the exact time the game ended because then she'd know exactly when the Ford's headlights should appear, curving off of the highway and bouncing slowly up the lane toward the house. She went to the window and leaned over the shelf of African violets to push aside the sheer curtain. The rain seemed to have stopped, but the tree limbs outside were coated with a glaze that reflected blue-white from the mercury vapor yard light on its tall pole.

She was just bracing herself against images of Roxanne killed, of hearing from her television set "A one-car accident claimed the life of a Wadena teenager late Friday night. Icy road conditions were blamed for . . .", when she saw headlights bobbing in the lane. Thank God, low Ford headlights, not the high lights of Clete's pickup. Quickly she turned on the pole lamp and the television, and settled herself deeply in the brown fake-leather recliner. She was steady when Roxanne came in.

What she wanted to do was wrap her arms around the warm and pliable little girl with red crayon on her knee, hold her and say, "I'm not ever going to let you go." But there was no way Thora knew to hug this tall, hostile stranger.

"Were the roads bad?"

The stranger didn't answer.

"Were the roads bad?" she repeated, looking this time to see what mood was written on Roxanne's face. There was anger there. Why? Thora turned away, afraid the anger was for her and she couldn't take any more of it, not now, not when there were only a few more hours between them, to love each other.

She turned her face back toward the television screen and began talking about the weather. "I hope our roads aren't bad Sunday," she ended, trying to pull something more personal into the conversation.

Roxanne's voice came at her like bullets. "Sure you do. You might have to keep me around a few more days if we get snowed in. You might have me underfoot a while longer, Mother. Well I promise you this, I'm leaving Sunday if I have to hitchhike to Des Moines, so you can rest easy on that point."

Thora turned and stared. My God, she thought, does Roxanne really think I want to get rid of her? Doesn't she *know*—

"Roxanne!"

And even then she wasn't braced for the fury of her daughter's words. "You sit there and let him say he's going to take my horse away. You never once came to watch me play. There was never anyone there watching me."

Thora sat wounded, long after Roxanne pounded up the stairs. The house grew quiet except for the unheard voice of the television set. In her mind Thora walked upstairs and sat down beside Roxanne and told her—what? That she loved her? Hard words to say when you had forgotten how, or never learned. That twice in Roxanne's sophomore year, when she played her first two home games, Thora had waited hopefully for some indication that Roxanne wanted her to come and watch; that Thora had gone anyway, driving the stock truck that frightened her, and stood in the doorway of the gym behind a screen of other watchers, and followed every movement of that wonderful girl out there in guard position, in her white satin uniform with the kelly green trim. That after that she had settled for listening at home on the radio

44

and feeling frustrated because Armstrong's name was mentioned so seldom during the play-by-play.

Could she walk up those stairs, Thora wondered, and sit down beside Roxanne and explain to her why Buck had to be sold? No. Not now. Not two days before the life Roxanne wanted was going to begin for her. That would be closing the door on the trap, locking the girl in as surely as Thora had been locked into the HiWay Mobile Home Park for twenty-two years.

The television voices began to irritate Thora beyond endurance. She heaved herself up out of the chair and turned it off, then parted the green Sears curtains that filled the broad doorway between living room and bedroom. It had originally been a back parlor, not a large room to begin with and reduced greatly by the addition of the bathroom back in the forties. Now there was just enough space left to walk edgewise between the bed and the dressers and wardrobes that lined the side walls. The bed was the same old walnut veneer that her mother had died in.

As she began to undress Thora mused, if I had cancer and were lying in this bed, would Roxanne give up her life in Des Moines to come back and take care of me? I don't know. Maybe not. But that's not a fair comparison, is it? All I gave up was what I hated. I never wanted to leave the farm in the first place, and Roxanne is champing at the bit to get away from here and make a life of her own. It would be a real sacrifice for her. And I hope she's never put to that test.

When her clothes were hung away in the wardrobe Thora went through a routine that had become so automatic it hardly required thought. Systematically she studied in the mirror the three small moles on her neck then, turning around, the moles on her back. Then without the mirror she cataloged each of the brown spots on her arms and legs. No changes. They were all in their familiar sizes and shapes. No cancer starting yet. She dropped her nightgown over her head and sat on the edge of the bed to roll the rubber band off of the end of her braid.

She brought the braid forward over her bosom and stroked it, blank-faced, blank-minded, until her fingers separated the strands. Eventually her eyes focused on them, the three ribbons of gray-brown hair lying beside one another on her chest, each strand separated from the others and yet still bent into the zigzags demanded by the shapes of its neighbors.

Like the three of us, she mused, smiling a little, sadly, at her fancy. Like me and Clete and Roxanne, held together all these years, shaping each other, and now—and now coming loose.

She pulled out the top rubber band and began to brush, brush, brush, brush. When she closed her eyes she could pretend the hair was still glossy brown and the skin was still fresh and the nose not yet ugly. She could pretend her freedom wasn't coming too late.

THREE

Roxanne was awake and up much earlier than usual but even so, Thora was in the kitchen already, with coffee started and the egg skillet warming.

"You're up early," Roxanne said.

"So are you."

Roxanne's tone was normal this morning, even a shade softer than normal. It was as much of an apology as she knew how to make, and it was enough. Thora smiled at her, over her shoulder. The bathrobe she wore was a Christmas present from Roxanne; it had been Roxanne's junior class sewing project in Home Ec. It was red quilted nylon with white lace around the collar and down the front. The lace wasn't sturdy enough to withstand the washing machine and dryer, so Thora washed it out in the bathtub every Saturday.

"What are you going to do today?" Thora asked as she set Roxanne's breakfast in front of her.

Roxanne pulled in a long breath. She had awakened a half hour ago with her mind made up about today, but she hadn't really thought it through yet. "I'm going to put in some fence."

47

Her mother looked at her, mildly startled. "That's a funny thing to be doing on your last day home, isn't it? How about your packing?"

"That won't take long."

They ate silently, then Thora said, "What fence?"

"I'm going to make a little lot on the east side of the barn, and run fence down along that little bit of lane to the hay field, so the calves can come up to the barn for feed and water. It'll save a lot of hauling in winter."

Thora nodded. They had talked about it before, Roxanne suggesting and Clete nodding and agreeing, then forgetting. "Seems like a funny thing to do with your last day, though."

"*Mmm.*" Roxanne sipped at her steaming coffee. She hadn't quite come to enjoy the taste of it yet, but she needed its strength and heat. Rushing through a big fencing job struck her, too, as an odd thing to be doing today. But it seemed necessary somehow. When she pictured the farm without her, Roxanne did not envision her father stepping into the gap she was going to leave. Her imagination cast Thora in the role of morning and evening bale-thrower, water-carrier, grain-pourer. A feed lot for the weaned calves would make it easier. Roxanne's mind went no deeper than that into her reasons.

She could hear her father's sleep-breathing, not quite snoring but the next thing to it. "He got home okay last night."

Thora nodded. "Must have been late. I was asleep. Roxanne?"

"What."

"I'm sorry about Buck. Does it mean a lot to you to keep him? We could probably work out—"

Roxanne shook her head and stood up. "No. He bought Buck for me, and if he wants to take him back, he can. I just think it's a pretty crumby thing to do, is all."

Thora's face softened, and Roxanne had to turn away from it, and from remembering what she'd yelled at her mother last night. She went down to the landing and began pulling on boots and coveralls and knit hat and work gloves. The fence. That was the thing, now. A big job, and only a few hours to do it. A kind of satisfaction came up in Roxanne. She felt as though if she dug into today's work as hard and as deep as she could, today could be stretched out indefinitely and the threat of Des Moines would go away.

She hurried through the morning chores, then got out the spade and post hole digger and went to work. The ground was frozen only an inch or so down, no problem for the blades of the post hole digger. With rhythmic *chunk-chunks* she jabbed the digger deeper and deeper into the earth and brought up satisfying big bites of soil between its double blades.

This is my kind of work, she thought. *This* is my kind of work. Not file-clerking in some office.

She began to sweat, from work and fear, both.

It was coming at her too fast. It was one thing to say, next November after we finish picking corn, I'm going to move to Des Moines and get a job and an apartment. It was something else to have that move coming tomorrow. She played the plan through her head again and again.

Leave early in the morning, Mom driving. Stop along the way for a copy of the Des Moines *Sunday Register*. Read the want ads on the way, and pick out three or four rooms-for-rent ads, and study the help-wanteds. Get to Des Moines, try to get me a room in a rooming house or someplace like that, close to downtown so I can look for jobs. Then first thing Monday, go to the State Employment Agency because they don't charge a fee, answer ads from the paper, try my darnedest to get myself hired somewhere as soon as I can.

Survive.

Prove I can.

And then—

But it was bleak, thinking beyond the next few months. Her imagination fell short of conceiving a pleasant life in Des Moines, a life that would fit around Roxanne Armstrong and make her feel comfortable. Like here.

She shook her head and drilled her attention into her work.

Before lunch time Roxanne had a more than satisfying morning's accomplishment stretched out behind her, an L-shaped string of post holes ten feet apart, three feet deep, in a tidy line out from the corner of the barn, then back north all the way to the hay field fence. She looked back at them and smiled. The rest would be easy, just setting the posts and stringing the wire. It occurred to her to wonder whether her father might be angry at her going ahead with the fence. It was his farm, after all.

To heck with him, she decided. And she decided something else. If he was going to sell Buck tonight, okay, but he wasn't going to have it easy.

She propped her tools against the barn and went around to the other side, stopping along the way for her bridle. Buck was still near the barn in the yearlings' lot, hoping for a little more hay before he wandered down into the pasture.

"One last ride, old buddy," she told him. Boots rose from her bed in the machine shed and came trotting up. She knew what "ride" meant. Using the edge of the feed bunker for a stirrup, Roxanne settled herself onto Buck's woolly back and reined him away from the buildings in case her father was watching from the window. They followed the foot-wide cattle path that wound between thickets of brush and sapling elms, Buck ambling along at his comfortable single-foot, Boots trotting behind, sniffing.

It wasn't a long ride. She didn't want to look at those familiar red ears very long, or think about not ever sitting on this back again. She led him through a sagging metal gate at the far end of the pasture, then slipped off his bridle and turned him loose. He had almost forty acres to get lost in now, rough land and dense underbrush along the river. It might take Clete an hour to find him. With sour satisfaction Roxanne pulled the gate shut and watched Buck trot heavily away toward the cows.

An hour's worth of work after lunch, setting heavy

wood posts into the holes and tamping them firm, then stringing barbed wire from a giant spool and securing it to the posts with heavy staples, and the fence was done. Stupid of us, she thought as she put the tools away, working our butts off all these years with that extra carrying, when a morning's worth of work would have taken care of it. But that's the way he runs this place. Always has. I get a good idea and he ignores it, because I'm a kid, according to him, and yet he never thinks of anything himself. He doesn't care about this place. Let the fences fall down, let the barn door fall off. What does he care? He'll get in his pickup and toodle off to town, or the sale barn, come home drunk, sleep half the next day.

He doesn't care about this place.

I do. I love it. Damn, I don't want to leave it.

It isn't fair, me going and him staying. What's going to become of things around here?

She paused at the corner of the barn and gave the rough boards a pat, then looked around quickly to be sure no one saw her. Good-bye, barn. Two of its sides were painted chocolate brown; Roxanne's idea, Roxanne's labor over the summer months, between hay cuttings and other more pressing work. Thora had come out several afternoons and picked up the extra brush, and helped the brown along. Another summer would have finished up the other two sides. Then, white doors and window trim. No. Roxanne shook her head. Quit thinking about it.

As she crossed the backyard toward the house, Roxanne passed Clete heading out toward the ma-

52

chine shed. Going to get out the stock truck, she thought, so he can take my horse away and sell him. Who gets the money, Father dear, you or me? They passed without speaking.

At the back door landing Roxanne met her mother, headed toward the basement with an armload of sheets for the washer. "Go ahead," Thora said.

"No. Go ahead." When Thora had safely navigated the stairs Roxanne said, "Mom? Norma and Alene want to take me out for supper tonight, for a sort of a good-bye party. You don't care, do you?" It occurred to her suddenly that her mother might care.

Thora's voice sounded hollow, echoing up from the washer she was filling with sheets, hollow but not harsh. "That's all right. That'll be nice for you. Alene home for the weekend, is she?"

"I guess so."

"Who's going to drive?"

"I said I would if I can get the car. Is that okay?"

"Yes, okay. I trust your driving more than the others. Well, Norma is probably careful. I don't know about Alene, though, so I'd just as soon it was you driving."

Roxanne loved that woman down there in the basement. She loved her hard and suddenly, and she wanted to cry, but she wasn't accustomed to crying, certainly not just because her mother said she trusted Roxanne's driving.

So instead of crying, or going down the stairs and saying, I love you, Mother, Roxanne said, "The roads should be okay by now. The ice is melted off the trees, so I'm sure it's off the highways, and we won't be going on any back roads or anything like that. Probably just up to West Union or Elkader for supper. We might bowl a few games, or whatever they want to do."

"You'd better get your packing done this afternoon, then, hadn't you? We'll be leaving first thing."

"Yeah, I know, I'm going to do it now. It won't take long. I don't have that much stuff."

The washer started its swishing humming noises. Thora called above it. "I put the two suitcases in your room, and a good big cardboard carton. If you need more, let me know."

The suitcases in her room were the biggest and smallest of the three matching bags that were stored behind the bed in the spare bedroom. Why just two, she wondered? I could have used that middle-sized one, too, and then maybe I wouldn't have to use the cardboard box.

As it turned out, two suitcases and the box were just about right; small suitcase for tooth stuff and hair stuff and skin stuff, pajamas and slippers, big bag for the bulk of her clothes, at least the few clothes she judged correct for an office worker, a few skirts and two jumpers and a dress, some blouses and a couple of sweaters. Her best two pair of corduroys for weekends and evenings, and sweatshirts and flannel shirts. They could make her wear dresses at work, but in the privacy of her own room, by God, she was going to be herself.

The box held her clock radio, horse statues, high

school yearbook trained to open at the pages with the pictures of the basketball team, a few books she didn't want to leave, photo album mostly starring Buck, two pair of boots and, crammed into the leftover spaces, her pillow and a multicolored afghan crocheted by her Grandma Braun.

Sighing, Roxanne stood up and moved slowly around the room, stopping by the window. No way to stuff an eighty-acre farm into a cardboard carton, was there?

The stock truck was still parked by the barn. All this time, and he still hadn't caught Buck. That old horse must be running Dad all over the darned river bottom. Good. Good for you, Buck, don't you let him catch you easy.

One of the things Roxanne liked about Norma was that Norma was even taller than she was and didn't need to be stooped down to, like Alene. Another nice thing about Norma was that she never showed you her pictures unless you asked. Roxanne always asked.

They stood in the little alcove just off the Zimmerman dining room, Norma and Roxanne and Mrs. Zimmerman, looking at a partially completed watercolor of a snowy landscape, a jag of fence, and a pair of snow-blown horses.

"It's the November assignment for my course," Norma said. "We're on watercolor now, and I have to do one large winter scene and four small studies, one still life, one animal, and two of my choice."

"If they were going to assign you a snow scene," Mrs. Zimmerman said, "they should have waited till January or February when you could do it from life. How do they expect you to remember clear from last winter how those colors are on the snow?"

"It's really good, Norm," Roxanne said. It was what she always said, and it was what she always meant.

She let her eyes wander around this familiar house, saying good-bye to this part of her childhood. It was a bigger and better house than her own, with the floors entirely covered with shaggy green carpet, and early American furniture with colonial print and maple arms. No oil stove smelled up the living room in this house; no sir, there was a gas furnace in the basement, properly out of sight. The walls of all the rooms held Norma Zimmerman paintings and one painting, the one over the davenport, even had its own light above it. It was a long, long picture, almost as long as the davenport, a view of two farmsteads along a country road, at twilight, with the lights from the houses and barns brightening the quiet blues and grays. Roxanne loved it more than any of Norma's others because the two homes were hers and Norma's. The artist had taken some freedom, geographically, because the two farms were actually two miles apart, with other places between them.

Mr. Zimmerman was sunk deep into his colonial print recliner in front of the television set. The five-thirty news contained the market reports, and he had never missed it, not in Roxanne's memory. He was a large man, quiet and pleasant, whose life was happily filled with his farm, his quarter horses, and his daughter the artist. The older children, now grown and gone, had received equal pride and attention in their turns. Roxanne used to pretend he was her father and that she was just out on loan to the Armstrongs because they needed help with the farm work.

He ceased trying to light his pipe as Roxanne came into the living room. "Well, Roxy, so you're flying the coop tomorrow, huh?"

"It looks that way." She sat on the arm of a chair.

He smiled. "You don't sound overly thrilled about it."

She shrugged. Impossible to try to explain the violent mixture of her feelings to him. To anyone. To herself even.

"Our Norma's going to be mighty lonesome around here, without her sidekick. Why don't you give up all this nonsense about moving to Des Moines, and stay here with your friends where you belong?"

Mrs. Zimmerman came in and stood behind Roxanne, her hands squeezing Roxanne's shoulders. "Now Father, that's just foolish talk. Our Roxy's got to try her wings, just like all youngsters should. Just like Normie will be, come spring. You wouldn't want Normie hanging around here indefinitely, would you, when it comes time for her to start making her own life? Of course not."

The look on the man's face said with painful clarity that that was exactly what he would like. Roxanne saw it and looked away. Comparisons hurt too much.

Her own father would have Buck at the sale barn by now. Maybe he'll rent out my room, she thought bitterly, make a few bucks that way.

Norma was at the door, wrapped up and ready. Roxanne stood up.

"You let us know how you're getting along, now," Mrs. Zimmerman said. "You're going to have a wonderful time in Des Moines, but we all hope you'll come back here when it comes time to settle down permanently. You're like one of our own daughters, you know."

Roxanne bent down awkwardly for the hug, and muttered something that sounded like, "You, too," and hurried Norma out the door.

In the car, bumping out the lane toward the highway, Norma said, "Don't mind them. They get pretty mushy sometimes. How are your folks taking it, now that you're on the verge of leaving?"

Roxanne snorted. "Very well. Mom hasn't said three words about it except for what I should pack, and my dear father is out tonight selling my horse. He couldn't wait till I was gone, to make a little beer money for himself selling my things."

"Oh Rox, you're kidding. He's selling Buck? He can't do that. Buck is your horse."

"That's what I said. Fat lot of good it did me. Let's don't talk about it. It makes me too mad."

They rode in silence for a few miles, then Norma said, "Don't sell your mom short, though. I think there's a lot more to her than she lets on."

"Yeah, I know. She's okay. She just doesn't say much and sometimes—I don't know—I guess I need—"

"Yeah."

At the Wadena corner where the lighted cross shone down from atop the invisible bluff, they turned right and coasted down, past the high school and into town. Alene's house was just behind her father's gas station. She was waiting for them on the front steps. Alene didn't like to have anyone come inside her house, not even Norma and Roxanne.

Alene Taylor was too short to have been a basketball player for a school larger than Wadena Consolidated, but she had been an energetic and effective player. She and Roxanne had developed an ability to know just where the other was, and was going to be in the next few seconds on the court. This ability did a great deal to make up for Alene's lack of height and Roxanne's occasional lack of speed caused at times when her mind wandered to the people in the stands.

Although Alene was not tall enough to carry them well, she had large, heavy breasts and had for as long as Roxanne could remember her. Roxanne supposed they were the reason for Alene's loudly declared hatred of boys, her threat, in seventh grade, to kill Roxanne if Roxanne ever turned boy crazy. Roxanne was puzzled and angered by the threat at the time, but when she thought it over she decided that the sort of attention Alene's figure drew from the boys at school, the looks and the jokes, would probably be enough to make anyone hate boys. What was more puzzling was the way Alene began acting when boys were around, shrill and silly.

Alene climbed into the back of the car. "Hi, kiddies," she said, a little too loudly for the small, enclosed space. She had short frizzy hair of a dirty yellow color, and skin that was—unfortunate. She had graduated last spring with Roxanne, and had gone to Cedar Rapids to take a three-month course in business machines, but had quit after just a few weeks to take a job on an assembly line in a microphone factory. Better pay than office jobs, she'd told her friends back home, and more interesting co-workers. "Co-workers," as Roxanne and Norma understood it, was in the masculine gender.

Since tonight was an occasion they decided to bypass their usual hamburger stands and step up one degree. The Rathskellar. It was a cavelike cellar under the old hotel in Elkader, with a bar and juke box in front, and scarred, varnished tables in little niches against the rock walls at the back. Pizza was the only dish served.

When their drinks came, two Pepsis and beer for Alene, Norma raised her glass to Roxanne. "Here's to Roxanne, off to seek her fortune in the big city. Good luck."

Roxanne opened her mouth to reply.

"She's going to need it, too," Alene said. "You're in for some shocks, boy, when you start living on your own. When I started my job and they told me, you know, five hundred a month salary, that doesn't sound too bad, right? I figure I can live on that, get an apartment with some other girls, maybe a hundred a month rent, and all the rest just to live on, and with all the dates I was having I figured I wasn't going to have to spend much for food, just get taken out for dinner a lot. Well, that part's okay, but that five hundred a month? Turned out to be three-eighty."

Roxanne stared. "What happened to the rest of it?"

"Withholding. Social security. Company insurance."

"That much, huh?" Roxanne felt fear. How could anybody live on small beginners' salaries if they took out that much before they even gave it to you? "Maybe companies pay more in Des Moines, since it's a bigger city."

Alene shook her head. "I don't think so, and your rent will be higher."

Maybe Cedar Rapids would have been a better choice, Roxanne thought. It's smaller, and closer to home. No. Alene was already there.

Norma looked directly at Roxanne, as though to steer the conversation back to her with the force of her eyes. "Do you have any ideas about where you're going to apply first?"

Roxanne shrugged. "The big insurance companies probably. I've heard they're almost always hiring."

"Forget insurance companies," Alene said flatly. "They don't pay worth a darn, and they've got ten single girls for every single guy. You'll never beat those odds, Rox. You should try to get into some small company where they've got like a plant or factory of some kind, and only a few girls in the office."

"I'm going for a job, not a husband, Alene," Roxanne snapped.

"Hah. Tell me another, Mother. Listen, speaking of men, I've got big news I've been saving to tell you guys—"

The pizza arrived, a giant Supreme with everything. Roxanne took a slice and watched the cheese strings stretch out and out until they snapped and hung dripping oily sauce against the back of her hand. She was suddenly hungry. Breakfast had been hurried and lunch had been early. Now, at last, food and time to enjoy it, and friends instead of parents to be eating with. From now on that's the way it's going to be, she realized. Meals alone or with some friend she hadn't met yet. Maybe even dates. Dinner with a date, at some big fancy Des Moines restaurant. I can't go on being dateless forever, she thought.

"Roxy." Alene's voice demanded her attention. "Come back to the land of the living. Don't you want to know what my big news is?"

"Sure." The pizza was cool enough for a bite now. Roxanne savored it, knowing Alene's big news was going to be much more interesting to Alene than to anyone else.

"I, Alene Marie Taylor, am"—she leaned forward and whispered—"no longer a virgin."

Roxanne and Norma leaned forward, too, till the three heads were close over the pizza. "You're kidding," Roxanne whispered back. "Tell us all about it."

"Well." Alene gloried in the attention that was very clearly hers. "His name is Roger, and he works there at Turners with me only he's in the shipping department, and he's taken me out four times now so I guess we're more or less going together."

"I should hope to kiss a duck," Norma muttered.

"So anyway, he's got this van, see, with a bed, well not really a bed, it was a pile of sleeping bags actually, but it seemed like the honeymoon suite at the Hilton, I'll tell you girls." She closed her eyes and smiled.

"Get to the good part," Roxanne said, and Norma asked, "Where was all this honeymooning taking place, if I may ask?"

"At the parking lot at the airport."

Norma exploded with suppressed laughter. "You're kidding. The parking lot at the airport? Weren't you afraid of getting caught?"

"At that point," Alene said dreamily, "we weren't thinking about anything but—what we were doing. And besides, Roger said no one ever checks out there. Watching the submarine races, he called it."

"Never mind about that," Roxanne insisted. "Get to the good part. What was it like? Did you like it?"

"Kids, it was fantastic. It was the most fantastic—"

As the details poured out, Roxanne listened at first eagerly, then less and less eagerly, and finally with yawning boredom. The first time through, it was fascinating. Maybe even the second time. After that, no. She let her imagination carry her forward to the time and place ahead of her, to the choices she was going to have to make in case some man, some time, did want her body. She smiled ruefully at the thought of anybody wanting it. Thick ankles and heavy hips, so she looked knock-kneed even though she wasn't. The rest of her was okay, not bad anyway, and she didn't have a spectacular chest like Alene's, but it was probably passable. Certainly Roxanne had all the necessary urges. Boy, did she.

She began to wish Alene would shut up.

When the pizza was gone and the story finally finished, they went to the bowling alley and bowled a few games. Roxanne was subdued, full of last-time feelings, and Norma was her usual quiet self, so it was Alene whose shrillness attracted the attention of the four young men in the next lane. They were local boys, a few years out of school; one or two of them were mechanics of some sort, Roxanne thought. The others she didn't know.

What she did know, in spite of her lack of experience in these things, was that there was a pickup in the making. Who was picking up whom, she wasn't sure, but when Norma caught her eye and shook her head slightly, Roxanne agreed. In the end Alene moved to the other lane, and Norma and Roxanne went home.

When they were settled in the car and heading out of town Norma made a sound somewhere between a sigh and a laugh. "This wasn't exactly the send-off party I had in mind for you, Rox."

Roxanne smiled. "That's okay. It was fun anyway. It was educational, for sure. Do you think she really did it, or was she making it up?"

"I wondered that, too, at first, but all those details. No, I don't think Alene has got that much imagination. Can you imagine, though, losing your virginity in the back of a van at the Cedar Rapids airport? God."

"There must be a better way," Roxanne said. And I sure hope I find it, she added to herself.

They said their good-byes in the car at Norma's house; not good-byes, just, "See you at Christmas," and Norma said, "Rox? Listen, you're going to do great in Des Moines. I've got complete confidence in you, buddy."

"Yeah. Me too. See you."

She drove home thinking, Well, this is it. Saturday gone, and nothing left now but *the* day. Boy, I wish this was over.

FOUR

It was four o'clock by the time Buck was caught and loaded into the stock truck. Clete glanced at the house as he eased the truck into gear. Roxanne was out of sight. He let his breath out, relieved. He couldn't shake the feeling that he was taking something from his girl that he had no right to take, and it wasn't the horse. Not exactly.

Again he saw the stocky little twelve-year-old in her seersucker pajamas, felt her arms around him for that brief instant. Clete's throat swelled.

What went wrong?

What went wrong with all of it, with his whole life?

Well, it ain't over yet, he reminded himself. Fifty-two isn't the end. There's still time. Maybe.

He turned onto the highway, but not toward the sale barn. There was something that had to be done first, much as Clete would have liked to avoid it.

He took the blacktop toward Fayette, toward his father's place. It was a ridge road following the crests of the land. On either side of the truck's windows the landscape rolled down and away in undulating browns and greens and cornfield creams, to the violet blue of the distant hills. Clete seldom noticed such things, but this was a leave-taking day and he was suddenly aware of the quiet beauty which would soon be replaced by a city, a factory.

He left the blacktop for a narrow gravel road, then for an even narrower one. Here the hills and the oak woods closed in around him. Houses became small and poor, and frequently empty. As the truck crossed a small stream, a fox lifted his head from the water and watched. Rounding a blind curve in the road, Clete braked suddenly and waited for a family of deer to amble across the road and pour themselves over the fence and disappear into the timber beyond.

His father's house appeared, a flimsy structure covered with tan fake-brick tarpaper. It sat close to the road in a wooded hollow, and flanking the house, like piglets around a sow, were scattered junk-car bodies, each housing a pair of coon hounds on chains.

Clete parked the truck, but didn't get out. The house was dark, and from where he sat Clete could see that Major's chain was empty. That meant that Dad and the dog were gone already, disappeared into the timber probably for the rest of the night. Impossible to find them.

Relief filled and lightened Clete. "I tried," he thought. "Can't do no more than that."

It would have been impossible anyway, to try to make the old man understand why Clete was leaving. To leave a good farm, an easy life, to go work in a factory, that was something old Malcolm would never comprehend. Giving up a good life like that just because there was no love in it for you. Because that little girl was better at running the farm than you were, yourself. A man had to be needed, damn it.

Well, just wait till he was gone, and Roxanne, too. Then see if Thora could run that place by herself. Not even she could manage that. She'd see how much she needed him, after he was gone. She'd come after him, ask him to come back. With Roxanne gone—

In the distance, Major gave voice and all the hounds in the yard came out of their car bodies and howled in answer. Clete watched them, and his eyes and attention wandered to the house. He'd grown up here, from the time he was three, and the family had come up from Arkansas to escape the depression.

His mother had died the year before, mostly from malnutrition, and left the four children, Roy, Melvin, Cletus, and the baby girl, Ruthie. The family finally settled here, on this tiny, unproductive backroads farm that was available on shares and needed no cash investment.

The Armstrongs settled into the farm, but never quite into the community. They were different from their neighbors, and young Clete soon began to realize it. Everyone was poor, but the other families he came to know were poor in a neater way, somehow. They worked hard at things like keeping fences repaired, things that never bothered Malcolm much. They kept their gardens weeded and their buildings painted if they could any way afford paint. Children were scrubbed and nosewiped and spanked when they needed it.

Malcolm Armstrong seemed to feel that, once having landed his family in this superior place, he could relax and spend his time acquiring coon hounds, which he kept chained to junked car bodies. When young pigs slipped through his rusted fences and were run over on the road, Malcolm took it philosophically. There were plenty of pigs. And if Ruthie and the boys spent more time splashing around in the clear, sand-bottomed river than they did hoeing the garden, well, kids were only young once; it was nice they could enjoy it.

The land was farmed, but only enough to pay the farm's owner his stipulated minimum. It was just a small hillside farm, not one that many sharecroppers would have wanted, so the Armstrongs were allowed to stay. The buildings were already ramshackle, so they didn't change drastically under Malcolm's lack of care.

Malcolm, and gradually the two older boys, became more and more engrossed in the coon hounds and the all-night hunts, and the drinking that was necessary in order to survive and enjoy the night-long chases up hills, through dense woods and over barbed wire fences after the caroling hounds.

Cletus was never much interested in coon hunting, but neither was he much interested in school, or in the farm. He did a little work around the place because he could see the relationship between keeping the hogs penned and food on the table next winter, between giving the garden vegetables at least a fighting chance against the weeds, and having enough to eat. But he resented the fact that he was just about the only one doing any work, and so he never kept at it very long at a time.

He was a tall, narrow boy, with the sandy coloring so common to his Ozark background. He was polite and pleasant and generally easygoing, and he did more thinking about the future than all of the other Armstrongs put together, with the exception of Ruthie, who began early to scheme for a marriage that would insure an easy life. Clete's goal was similar, although he was still exploring ways and means.

After tenth grade he quit going to school. His father didn't much care whether he stayed in school or not; in fact, Malcolm was rather of the opinion that two more years of education would be pretty much wasted on a farmer anyway, and Clete would be better off at home, taking over the farm work so that he and Roy and Mel could give more of their time and energy to earning money from coon bounties. His logic didn't stretch to include the fact that the bounties they earned came nowhere near covering the bills at the liquor store.

But Clete was beginning to learn a thing or two about himself, and one thing he learned was that he didn't like being looked down on as one of those shiftless Armstrongs. Although he loved to laze away an afternoon on the front porch, cleaning a rifle that didn't need it, he bristled at the thought of being considered lazy.

What he needed was to get out on his own, to find a way of making it through life in a comfortable, pleasant way that did not include spending long, broiling July days on a hay wagon with chaff down his back, nor wading through knee-high snow on a twenty-below-zero morning to carry water buckets to pigs. Sometimes he felt himself slipping toward the habits of his father and brothers—Just don't worry about tomorrow. Go coon hunting tonight and you'll sleep all day tomorrow anyhow, and you won't need to worry about food on the table, or making the sharecrop minimum.

But Clete was brighter than the others, bright enough to see ahead and to realize that some day there might be no more pigs to butcher or beans to pick. He didn't want to live under that kind of insecurity. No sir, security had grown to be an important part of what Cletus considered a comfortable life. A pay check. That was the thing.

He managed to talk his way into a part-time job in the gas station in Wadena. His paychecks were very small but he enjoyed the work and the feeling of command that came with the uniform. When people drove in, he was their host and in a sense their superior. They were in his station, after all, asking *him* for things like "check the oil" and "which way is the rest room?" What was more important, the gas station, being the only one in town, was the social center for

71

several men and boys who had the time and inclination to hang around. Evenings, the gas station and the tavern were the only places open, and hanger-outers drifted from one place to the other, so that all the news that got talked about in the tavern also got talked about at the gas station. And Cletus Armstrong was in the big middle of it.

He had begun thinking seriously that this was his place in life, when something better came along. The war. It seemed better anyhow until he was in it, and then it was too late to change his mind. The idea of all that pay with no living expenses was what drew him into the recruiting office. Two years of living off of the government and banking his paychecks, he figured, would set him up in a position to buy a little gas station of his own when he got out. That was the big dream just then, a station of his own in some little town like Wadena, car-crazy high school boys to do most of the work, and Cletus Armstrong to do most of the profit-reaping.

During the next two years he forgot about that gas station. He forgot everything except fear; first it was fear of his sergeant and all the pyramiding power behind him, then it was fear of being killed, of being horribly wounded, of having to kill. His thoughts became a running prayer for survival although he had no particular belief in God. When the paychecks came they melted away within a few days for the drinking and gambling that took his mind temporarily away from the nearness of death.

At the end of the two years Clete came home,

much much older and somewhat more sophisticated, but with no money and no clear idea of what he wanted. What he didn't want, though, was the farm and his father's way of life. Melvin was off in the navy, Roy was home after a brief time in the army, mustered out because of severe color-blindness. Ruthie was gone, into a marriage that seemed, to Clete anyway, no better than the life she'd led at home. Malcolm seldom shaved any more, or made any attempt to clean up around the house. The live-stock was gone and all that was left proliferating were the coon hounds. There were more than thirty of them now. Newly junked cars had been hauled in to house them.

No, Clete told himself after just a half-day back home, he could never go back to living like this. The army had accustomed him to neatness and some de-gree of order. Army food wasn't good, and it was served on tin plates, but at least the plates didn't have rims of old food growing mold around their edges.

Although the Armstrong farm disgusted him now, Clete found unexpected waves of pleasure going over him as he walked the roads of the Volga valley, from Wadena to Volga City. This was a bright green and blue place, with birds and squirrels and calves and roosters, no gunfire or exploding land mines or bloody limbs blown off of friends three feet away. A good place for a man to settle down, he decided. Yes, settle down, find a nice, warm, admiring wife, a job of some kind.

A job. But what kind? He knew a little about farming, a tiny little about gas stations, and more than he wanted to know about wars. He tried the gas stations first, but they were all doing slim business. Gas was rationed, rubber for tires was almost nonexistent, and many of the local farmers had gone back to horses both for farm work and for transportation to town and back.

He thought, as he walked the country roads, about going to Waterloo or Cedar Rapids or even Des Moines. Jobs should be plentiful, with so many men away in the war. That might be the thing to do. A regular job and a regular paycheck, and a whole city full of girls whose men were gone. He had almost made up his mind to do that when another possibility occurred to him.

A nice young widow with a good farm and no one to run it for her. As fast as men were being killed off overseas, Clete figured there were bound to be a few well-set widows around these valleys. A farm of his own, where he would be boss. Now there was a pleasant possibility—to succeed where his father had failed. To show the people around here that all the Armstrongs weren't shiftless Arkie hillbillies.

And farm prices were good now. The war had created an ample market, and it didn't take much of a farm to make a comfortable living. Clete's mind began to pick up speed. If a man had beef cattle instead of dairy he wouldn't be tied to all that morning and evening milking. In fact, during the winter there'd be hardly any work to do at all. A good solid

74

house around him, an adoring wife to keep the place clean, a few little sandy-haired boys to follow him around and pester him to teach them things, to tell them about the war. Yes. A good life. Some hard work spring and fall, and some haying in summer, but he could put up with that, knowing that it was his farm, and he was boss, and knowing that all winter he could laze around in the warm house, or spend his afternoons and evenings in the tavern or on the bench in front of the gas station.

These thoughts were solidifying in Clete's head one August afternoon as he rode on the tailgate of a stock truck on the Volga City–Wadena road. The truck was going slowly over the sun-hardened ruts of the dirt road, so the three bred cows inside wouldn't be jarred too badly on their way to the sale barn.

Because of the truck's slow speed Clete had time to see the girl hoeing vegetables, even though the farmstead sat well back from the road behind a narrow corn field. Even from that distance Clete saw her youth, her size and sturdiness. Almost without conscious thought he slipped off the tailgate and stood looking. A good farm, he thought, not a showplace but the barn was big and the place seemed well enough cared-for. Not so well cared-for, though, as to mean there were ample men around the place. He smiled. The house was medium-sized for that area, square, white, two stories, solid enough but not fancy. He nodded. It would suit him. Now to find out what the situation was. The name on the mailbox was Braun. He seemed to recall some boys named Braun in school, but that was so many years ago he couldn't be sure.

"I'll ask for a job," he decided as he started up the lane. "That'll be the best way to find out if she's got a husband or brothers. If not, and if she should hire me, and if the place is hers or is going to be hers, then—"

He stopped at the edge of the garden and looked at the girl. Although Clete hadn't done enough thinking about marriage to have a very firm idea of what he wanted, he had somehow imagined himself with a little wife, someone who would have to stretch up to kiss him. Someone who, because she looked up to him physically, would just naturally develop the habit of looking up to him in all ways. The ideal would have been someone who had married young, to a bum who mistreated her but who died after just a few months of marriage and left her with his farm, or at least a hefty insurance settlement. Then Clete would come into her life and be gentle and good, by comparison, and her love for him would be complete and instantaneous, and would not need to be earned by continuous goodness to her in later years.

This girl didn't fit the physical measurements he had in mind, Clete thought in that split second of eyes meeting eyes, and yet he liked her. She hadn't even said hello yet, but he liked her plain, pleasant looks and the soft brown waves of hair that blew around her face. He even felt himself liking the bigness of her. It seemed sheltering.

But what struck him most forcefully was her expression, her look of fulfilled expectation, as though she had been waiting all her life for Cletus Armstrong to come into it. He felt intensely flattered.

He introduced himself politely and said he was just back from the war, and did she by any chance need a hired hand?

Need, yes, she told him, but afford? No. As she led him back toward the pump for a drink of water she explained that all three of her brothers had been killed overseas, and her parents had lost most of their will to work, so she was pretty much carrying the farm herself and needed help in the worst way, but there was just no cash to pay wages.

He smiled as he walked behind her toward the pump.

The courting began immediately, and since it was time for the third cutting of hay, Clete just naturally began spending his days at the farm, helping with the hay. The old man who was Thora's father welcomed him in an abstracted way, hardly ever focusing his eyes on Cletus, taking his help for granted.

Clete would have liked a little more appreciation but he didn't spend much energy worrying about old Gunnar. Thora was the key, here, and Thora was just about wrapped up and sold. She worked beside him on the hay wagon as they gathered the long, soft, green swatches from the fields and hauled load after load to the barn. The September haying had none of the unpleasantness of the July haying. The days were easy-weathered, sunny, breezy, designed to make a

77

man forget all about factories in Waterloo. Thora, too, was a complete pleasure. She was quiet, but he could tell she lit up inside when he was there. She looked at him as though he were the prize at the fair, and she listened to him as though he were wise.

It was going to be a good life.

It wasn't until after the wedding, when Clete was installed in the over-the-kitchen bedroom with Thora, installed in the farm and the family, that he began to know that the plan had soured somewhere along the line. The old people seldom spoke to him, and when they did it was to give him orders, what work was to be done that day, and how to do it. Hell, he thought resentfully, two years of taking orders from sergeants was enough. He didn't want any more of it. When he'd first met Gunnar and Elvira they had seemed to him to be frail, almost death-bound. Not likely to be around long. Now, on closer knowing, they seemed tough, leathery, ageless, and deathless.

He felt as though he were, once again, an unpaid farmhand, a child doing chores for parents, and he hated it.

The situation with Thora began to disintegrate, too, as the winter weeks went by. He felt as though once she owned him she lost interest in him. There were no fights, no uproars, just attention wandering away from him and back to the farm. The adoration that seemed to have been there before the marriage simply evaporated, or never existed in the first place, he wasn't sure which. Clete's two years in the Army had taught him about lovemaking, and that was one area

78

in which he was sure he excelled. And yet here he was, with a wife who appeared to prefer sleeping to making love. It galled him. What galled him further was the fact that Thora, with her bigness and her nonchalance, had the power to reduce him to impotence.

Nights were bad for Clete that winter, but days weren't much better. He did a little of the work, but with Gunnar in fierce control of the morning and evening milking, and Thora volunteering for the rest of the livestock chores, there wasn't much of a slot for him to fit into, not till spring, he thought bitterly, when they're going to work me like a plow horse. Well that's what they think.

He developed the habit of slipping off silently to places where he could be alone to think, usually one of the empty bedrooms upstairs. The room was unheated. There was even frost on the insides of the window panes. But Clete would wrap up in a heavy patchwork quilt from the bed, and sit on the cedar chest and think about his escape.

It was painfully apparent to Clete that he had made a mistake. Marrying Thora, whom he hardly knew, just for the security of her farm, was wrong for both of them. He said these words to himself often, but he never actually thought about Thora's side of it. What he thought about was that sweet little dependent wife that he'd always wanted and didn't get. He thought about living in Waterloo and having a regular job, something that he'd learn to do well, so the men he worked with would come to like him, respect

79

him. Maybe someday be foreman, with men under him.

And money in his pockets. Oh Lord, how he wanted money of his own. So many times this winter he'd wanted to go into Wadena and spend the long afternoons in the friendly warmth of the tavern with other farmers whose work was winter-stopped. But he was completely without money, couldn't have bought his own beer, much less rounds for the others, as he dreamed of doing.

Sitting on that cedar chest with the quilt around him, Clete Armstrong came to a decision. It was dumb to have made the mistake; it would be pure stupidity to ruin the rest of his life because of it. Waterloo was the place for him. And yet he didn't quite want to desert Thora. It wasn't so much the idea of losing Thora that bothered him, it was the idea of being the kind of man who walked out on his wife for no good reason, at least no reason the rest of the world would consider good. She wasn't unfaithful to him, that was for sure.

What he would do, he decided, was to announce to Thora that they were leaving the farm, moving to Waterloo. She would hate the idea, refuse to go, refuse to leave her parents without help for the coming work season. She would decide to stay here. The decision would be hers, not his. He would go to Waterloo, get his job, find a place to live that would discourage Thora from joining him if she were tempted to, something like maybe a trailer in a crowded trailer park. They would be separated, and eventually quietly divorced, and he would have the life he was always meant to have. Thora would find someone else, and they'd both be better off.

That was the original plan. When it backfired Clete shifted to an alternative version. Go ahead and live his life just as he wanted to and wait for Thora to get fed up with Waterloo and the trailer, and go back to the farm.

His job at the John Deere plant gave Clete everything he'd hoped for, money in his pocket, a good bunch of guys to work with, many from backgrounds similar to his own, and dignity. His job, spray-painting body parts of giant tractors as they came off the assembly line, was easy enough to do and do well, and Clete loved the security of knowing what each day was going to demand of him. Sometimes there were long delays on the assembly line, when they had to wait for more work to come through. Then there was nothing for him and his co-painters to do but sit around and tell jokes and feel pleased about the loafing time. Then it seemed to Clete that he had found just the life he'd been wanting all along.

He didn't even mind having Thora to support. She made few demands on him and she never complained about the increasingly long hours he spent at Jimmy's Tap with the other guys from the plant. As the years went by, Clete grew to depend on Thora more than he was aware. It was good to have a clean home to come back to, and someone to talk to when he felt like talking. He gradually forgot about hoping she would go back to the farm. He found an adequate

81

sex life among the women at Jimmy's, adequate to restore his belief in himself in that respect, at least. And no one came along whom he wanted to marry. So staying married to Thora was not uncomfortable in any important way.

The baby was a surprise. After so many childless years Clete assumed there would never be children, and he didn't give it much thought one way or the other. Then suddenly there was Roxanne. He was surprised at his own delight in having produced a child. It was fun to look into the crib when he came home late at night, and see that soft, pink little baby sleeping there under her yellow blanket.

As Roxanne grew older Clete would sit and hold her sometimes, and search her small face for signs of himself. There were none. She was Thora's offspring, one hundred percent. When the child squirmed away from him and scampered to Thora to be held, Clete hurt a little bit inside. So he joined the Sports Club and began to spend his weekends down there, shooting on the rifle range.

When the call came, announcing Elvira's cancer, Clete had little time to make his decision. Things had to be done quickly. Here was his chance to be free of his family, a chance he had waited for at least in the back of his mind, for twenty-two years. But now that he was faced with losing Thora and Roxanne he found that they had grown to be an important background for his life. He was used to thinking of himself as a family man now, and it felt comfortable to him. A twenty-four-year-old bachelor in Waterloo might have had endless fun, but a forty-four-year-old divorced man with a receding hairline and a diminishing interest in the women at Jimmy's? He wasn't so sure.

And there was the farm. It could be his now, to run as he wanted. The old dream, come to life again. Long winter days with nothing much to do. No time clock to punch.

And balancing the scale was Roxanne. She was ten now, and Clete hardly knew her. On the farm she would be with him all the time, asking him to teach her things, riding on the tractor with him, looking up to him. In his imagination, his daughter became the small adoring female of his old daydreams.

He decided to go to the farm, at least as long as Roxanne was at home, he told himself. As long as that little girl needs me, I'll stay. After that, it'll depend.

But once again things refused to follow Clete's plans for them. The farm was all right. Elvira died and Gunnar followed soon after, and the farm was in Clete's hands to run as he wanted. He sold the unprofitably small dairy herd and replaced them with beef cattle, which did well. Thora was softer and happier now that she was back where she wanted to be. But there were two big disappointments sticking in Clete's craw. One was that the Brauns had willed the farm to Thora, to be passed directly to Roxanne. Clete was excluded. Even though Thora allowed him to run the place his own way, there was still the knowledge between them that it was her farm. Hers and Roxanne's.

Roxanne was the other disappointment. She went her own way, exploring the farm and learning about it. If she had questions, she asked them of her mother. She had spent the first ten years of her life seeing Clete as a stranger who spent small fragments of time in their trailer. By now she had no curiosity about her father, no desire to get to know him.

Thora and Roxanne seemed to Clete to be a closed pair, a complete entity with no need for him prying in between them. So he took a job at the sale barn, helping out with the hog sales on Wednesday nights, cattle sales on Fridays, and horse sales one Saturday night a month. The paychecks were to be his to spend as he pleased. That was an unspoken understanding between him and Thora. They were small paychecks, but they bought him the long hours he loved, in the Wadena Tavern and in the sale barn café. Clete Armstrong was never known to be drunk. His consumption of beer after beer was entirely social. He was open-handed about buying rounds for the others, for whomever was in the tavern or the café, and he was generally well liked.

His life settled into a comfortable routine. There were women to flirt with at the sale barn, although straying wives and single women were few in this rural community, so the flirting seldom grew serious. But as the exterior of Clete's life became more comfortable, his awareness of being unloved began to swell. Thora didn't love him, never had, so far as he could tell. And neither did anyone else in the entire world, including his daughter. It was a bleak realization.

One Saturday night while Clete was lounging at the side of the sale ring, waiting for the endless pieces of tack and equipment to be sold so that they could get started on the horses, old Bill Stepp, who owned the sale barn, said, "Clete, you'd ought to get that girl of yours a horse. What is she, about twelve now? Every twelve-year-old girl wants a horse, Cletus. You'd ought to get her one. There's a nice little pinto gelding coming through tonight that's an awful nice kids' horse. My neighbors' kids had him and they could do anything with that horse."

The timing was right. Roxanne's twelfth birthday was coming up in a few days, and Clete had almost three hundred dollars in the bank, the most he'd ever saved in his life, intending to use it to finance a break with Thora and the farm, a return to Waterloo, when he was ready to go. And he'd been in an especially love-hungry mood lately, not sex-hungry, just wanting some affection. He thought about Roxanne giving him a big hug when he brought home that horse for her, Roxanne suddenly realizing how much he loved her and wanted her to love him. The horse would be the turning point. With a daughter who loved him, maybe he wouldn't want to go back to Waterloo.

But the horse plan backfired, too. One quick hug by the tailgate of the stock truck the night he brought Buck home, and after that Roxanne seemed to disappear. She was always off riding around the farm alone, or down the road with her friend. Sometimes when Clete and Roxanne were together, at mealtimes or in the living room in the evening, he would catch her looking at him in a way that was part expectant, part accusing, as nearly as he could read it. He didn't understand her and it angered him to feel that there was something she apparently expected from him, and he didn't know what it was. It made him feel dumb, the way Thora sometimes made him feel. Dumb, and then resentful.

He went back to avoiding the two of them, fading away into the basement or spare room when he could, and he began to dream again about the good life. Waterloo, the plant, the guys at Jimmy's Tap. The women at Jimmy's Tap. Coming back to the farm was a mistake; he could see it now. This was the right place for Thora and Roxy, but not for Cletus Armstrong.

The plans began again, in his head. Escape. Go back to Waterloo. But although the idea pleased him and gave him something to think about while he rode the tractor around the cornfield or sat staring on the cedar chest in the empty bedroom, he found that he was in no hurry to make the break. It was comfortable enough here, for now. The farm made a good enough living, and his nights at the sale barn were pure pleasure, joking with the men, flirting with the girls. And besides, it wouldn't look good for him to run out on his little girl. No, wait till Roxy's left home, he decided.

There'd be plenty of time to save a little money here and there from his sale barn pay, enough to live on in Waterloo till he could get back on at the plant and draw his first paycheck. Plenty of time. True, he hadn't begun saving until it was too late, and now that he'd gotten so firmly in the habit of spending everything that was in his pocket at the bar, he found he couldn't save. And when the time for him to leave came, there would be no way to get the necessary money except to sell the horse.

One thing Clete was sure of. This time he wasn't going to make the mistake of telling Thora what he was going to do before he did it. He was almost positive she wouldn't leave the farm again, and follow him to town, but he wasn't taking that chance. No, sir. Cletus Armstrong was fifty-two years old and, by God, if he was ever going to find that sweet little woman to love him it was going to have to be now. He was going to have to go alone.

Clete woke from his thoughts, to an awareness of passing time. He kicked the truck to life and, with one long look at his father's house, drove away.

"I'll write him a letter after I get to Waterloo."

He drove as fast as he could without toppling Buck on the curves, back toward Wadena and the sale barn. The lights were on at the barn, but the parking lot was still mostly empty. Clete backed up to the loading chute and led the horse down into the small intake enclosure. Along the back wall was a high enclosed booth, and behind its window Bill Stepp sat with his record book.

"Give us an early number, will you, Bill?" Clete asked. "Not too early though." He knew the first few horses to be auctioned usually brought low prices. Most buyers wanted to wait a while, see what else was coming. And the last horses usually went low, too. Most people had gone home, or already bought what they wanted.

Bill looked up at Clete and Buck. "That your girl's horse you got there? Well, I guess she won't be needing him now that she's leaving the nest, huh? Let's see, how old a horse is he now, twelve? He'd ought to bring a fair price, good solid kids' horse like Buck. Course, November's going to be a buyers' market for riding horses, but then you've been around here long enough to know that. Let's give him thirty-seven."

Bill handed down a shiny circle of paper with "37" on it, and Clete slapped it, gummed side down, onto Buck's rump just above his tail. He led the horse on through the fenced passageway into the main barn and tied him in one of the stalls. He stood for a moment, stroking Buck's mane, trying to get the ragged places to lie down. Clete had no particular fondness for animals beyond their market value, but he was struck by a sudden and unexpected remorse about Buck, about Roxanne, about all the years that had just somehow gotten by him. His little girl had stretched up and become a woman while he was still trying to learn how to talk to her.

. "That your horse?"

It was a woman's voice, behind him. Clete turned. After all his years of experience Clete had developed the ability to size up a woman as quickly as a camera takes a picture. This one made him go alert. She was standing in the stall door, moving her eyes from Buck to Clete, but with emphasis on Clete.

She was small but chesty, maybe thirty-five, maybe forty, reddish hair, lots of eye make-up, neat little butt packed into very tight Levi's, a western shirt whose pearl buttons almost failed to hold together in front. She wore a fleece-lined denim jacket like Clete's, open but hiding just enough to tantalize. Her eyes met Clete's and the look was warm.

Oh yeah.

"You interested in buying a horse?" he asked, making his voice deep and soft. "This'd be a good horse for your kids, good stock horse for your husband to go get the cows on. If that's what you're looking for."

She grinned, a slow, broad grin. "I'm not looking for nothing for my husband. That bastard can do his own looking. And I don't have any kids." She came in close and stroked Buck's face. "I'd like to try him out." Her voice was soft to match Clete's. He knew it wasn't the horse she was interested in, and he exulted.

"You got it, Red." He tossed the lead rope up over Buck's neck and gave her a boost up, adroitly getting

89

himself a handful of fanny in the process. She looked down at him and scowled but there was an obvious smile beneath it.

Too soon it was time for Clete to go to work. The horses and tack were beginning to come in now, and he had to help get everything logged and numbered. He carried the tack out into the sale ring and piled it around, so people could walk through and look it over. There were saddle blankets, water buckets, a few stock and pony saddles, a pony cart and harness, a crate of half-grown rabbits, and endless bits of leather and metal. While he worked the woman managed to stay within talking range.

Dixie, her name was. She was from over by Littleport. Her husband was a trucker and she was sick and tired of sitting home Saturday nights while he was supposedly laid-over on runs out of town, but she wasn't buying that line any more. She felt like getting out among-em tonight, and she loved horse sales, so here she was. Her words told Clete that much, and the way she brushed against him told him more.

The sale finally began. It was a small crowd, a slow night, and not much to sell. Fine with Clete. The sooner they were finished here, the sooner he could pocket his escape money, and get that hot little redhead out to his truck.

It didn't prove to be that easy. When the sale was finally over and Clete had tucked away in his pocket the two hundred from selling Buck, and his thirty for tonight's wages, plus the twenty Billy added when

Clete told him it was his last night, Dixie went with him willingly enough to the truck, but only to sit in the seat and neck and talk and drink from the bottle of scotch he had under the seat. He suggested, several times, that they'd be more comfortable in the back of the truck. She said no.

"I've got a better idea," she said when the scotch bottle was nearly empty. "You say you're taking off tomorrow for Waterloo. Okay. Take me with you. I've been trying to get away from that bastard I married for I don't know how long now, but he won't let me have a car, nor enough money to get away with. I had to borrow my neighbor's car to get here tonight. I was so desperate to get out of that house, you wouldn't believe."

"Oh yes I would."

"Well, okay then. Take me to Waterloo with you. It won't take me long to get a job. I've got lots of waitressing experience. We can get a place together for a while if you want, save expenses that way, and I'm a good little bed-warmer."

"I just bet you are." He reached for her but she caught his wrists.

"I am. But not in the back of a truck on a pile of horse shit. Well, is it a deal?"

"You bet your cute little tail it is. You tell me where you live and I'll pick you up some time around the middle of the morning. My wife and daughter will be leaving for Des Moines about nine, and I'll have to see them off. But after that—"

"No. Let's go tonight. Right now. Come on, Clete,

where's your guts? We've got money, and this truck, and each other. What else do we need? What difference does it make whether you leave Saturday night or Sunday morning, anyway?"

Clete thought about it. He liked the adventure in the idea. Just take off. Now. Be in Waterloo in a couple of hours, in bed, with Dixie. *Hooeee!*

But he hadn't planned to take the stock truck. Thora would be needing it. He'd planned to take the pickup or the Ford, whichever Thora and Roxy didn't take to Des Moines.

No. He couldn't quite let himself be the kind of man who would run off in the night, and not say good-bye to his one and only daughter. She might still give him that hug. She might even change her mind at the last minute and decide to stay home and be her dad's right-hand man on the farm—but no, he wouldn't be there.

He shook his head. Half a bottle of scotch was more than he was used to all at once. It was making him foggy.

"I'm sorry, Dixie," he said, being careful not to slur his words. "I have family responsibilities. Family responsibilities," he said again. It hadn't come out quite right the first time.

Dixie sat up straight and pulled her jacket around her. "Not half as sorry as you're going to be, buster, when you sober up and realize what you passed up." She got out of the truck and slammed the door.

Clete sighed.

FIVE

Breakfast was an almost silent meal. Roxanne had developed the habit long ago of eating whether or not she was hungry. It was stoking the machine with fuel, that was all. She was able to separate her digestion from her thoughts, so on this painfully final morning she was able to eat a full load of bacon and eggs and toast and coffee and the orange juice her mother had squeezed for her out of three fat oranges.

Everything in the kitchen seemed magnified, intensified, dearly familiar to her. Even her father's hangover after a sale night, although he was seldom up at breakfast time on such mornings. He hadn't said anything about Buck, and Roxanne didn't ask. She didn't want to know anything about it.

It was obvious to Roxanne that her father was hurting this morning. His eyes were bloody red and he winced at moderate noises and he ate nothing, just drank cup after cup of coffee. She had no sympathy at all for hangovers. They were fair payment in her opinion. But she understood that he was making an effort this morning to be upright, and it would have warmed her feelings toward him a little, at least around the edges, if she had let it.

In a careful voice, as though he might hurt himself if he put too much effort into it, Clete said, "Which car are you girls taking?"

"The Ford," Thora said, and Roxanne thought she heard an unusual gentleness in that voice, too. Why, she wondered?

Roxanne stood up. It was a quarter till eight, and her mother had said they should be on the road by eight. "I'll do chores, Mom, if you'll get my stuff loaded. It's just the two suitcases and the box."

Clete said, "Don't bother about the chores. I'll do them. You two want to get an early start. Here, I'll give you a hand with that box."

Thora stood, too. "I'll just do up the breakfast dishes."

"No, don't bother about them," Clete said. "I'll take care of them."

Roxanne and Thora both stared at him. To Roxanne's surprise, she saw her mother smile faintly. A look of unprecedented tenderness softened Thora's face. Roxanne looked away, confused. She was the one that was leaving, after all. What was going on between them?

She pulled on her coat, took a suitcase, and went outside to the car. Boots appeared from under the back steps and cantered gaily beside her. Saying good-bye to Boots almost made Roxanne break. She was still kneeling over the dog when Thora and Clete came out with the rest of her things. The car was loaded, and the three of them stood awkwardly beside its open doors.

To Thora, Clete said, "What time do you reckon to be back?"

"Eight or nine, I expect." Her voice was odd. Roxanne listened to it, puzzling.

Then Clete turned to Roxanne. He said nothing, just stood, his arms hanging loosely, his thumbs moving back and forth. He looked at her with a tenderness that Roxanne wasn't used to, from him, and didn't know how to receive. She waited for him to give her a good-bye hug; it seemed called for. But he didn't.

He said, "You be careful now. About men. You know."

She looked away from him.

He went on. "And you write to your mother every week."

"I will."

Thora finally broke things by pulling in her breath and saying, "Hop in, Roxy, let's be on our way."

Boots chased the car, not just out of the yard as she usually did, but all the way out to the highway and a quarter mile down it.

"She knows I'm leaving, Mom." Roxanne watched, worried that Boots might be hit by another car, until the dog slowed, turned, and trotted home.

They drove among the familiar hills and valleys, Roxanne memorizing with her eyes, and Thora staring straight ahead, her face expressionless. It wasn't until they were out of the hill country and cruising through flat farmland, richer than their own but without the beauty of the hills she knew, that Roxanne pulled her gaze and her thoughts together.

This is it, she told herself. The beginning of the big adventure. I'm going to get a toehold in that town, and I'm going to hang on. And probably in a few years I'll marry some nice young guy who works in some office, and I'll have kids and all that. And we'll come up to the farm for visits.

She made no sound, but her face was wet in streaks when her mother glanced at her.

In a careful voice Thora said, "Roxanne, you know you don't have to go."

"Yes I do."

"Is it what you want?"

Roxanne couldn't answer. She didn't know how to tell her mother that leaving the farm was the exact opposite of what she *wanted,* and that was a big part of why she had to. It didn't make enough sense even to Roxanne, to try to explain to anyone, least of all to her mother. If she'd said, "I have to prove I can do it," her mother would come back at her with good logical arguments, and undermine Roxanne's strength, and right now she couldn't take that.

"Yes. It's what I want."

Thora looked away again. "Then you've got to do it. I don't want you, ever, to compromise, Roxanne. Do you hear me?"

The harshness in Thora's voice made Roxanne stare.

Thora said, "Promise me that one thing, and it's

the only promise I'll ever ask of you. You study hard at finding out what you want out of this life, and then you hold out for it, and don't settle for anything less."

The hum of their tires changed pitch as they slowed behind a lumbering, towering corn picker on the highway ahead of them. Thora could have passed, but she stayed behind it until it turned into a field access. It seemed to Roxanne that her mother was in no big hurry to get to Des Moines.

"Is that what you did, Mom? Compromise?"

Thora was silent for a long time. "Yes, in a way."

"When you married Dad?"

The lack of answer was answer enough.

"What did you want, instead of him? Did you want to get away from the farm?"

"No." That answer was firm. "No, I expect the farm was what I always wanted."

"Well, you've got it, haven't you?"

Thora gave her a long, kind look, as though there were things she wanted to explain, and couldn't.

Roxanne pressed. "What did you want, then, that you didn't get?"

Thora smiled. "Oh, nothing important, I guess. A man in a blue plaid shirt. Nobody real, just an idea I had of the kind of man I thought I'd marry."

"Then why did you marry Dad?"

Thora's smile stayed on her face, but it saddened. "I don't know, honey. It seemed like the thing to do at the time. I thought he loved me. Maybe I even thought I loved him, for a while there."

Roxanne wanted to back away now. This was getting too close. She wasn't used to talking to her mother about anything more personal than the egg count from the hens. But she wanted to know, too. She needed to know. She felt suddenly as though she were a repeat of her mother, starting over again with a new life, and it was crucial that she know what mistakes to avoid.

"It didn't work out very well, did it?" she asked gently. It felt funny, using a gentle voice with her mother, as though she were the strong one all of a sudden.

Thora looked at her, and the look was heavy with love. "It hasn't been a world-beater of a marriage. I'm not going to lie to you. But it gave me the one thing that means more to me than anything else in the world."

"Your farm?"

"No. My daughter."

They both looked away.

The two-lane highway became a four-lane, which eventually became Interstate 80, and by noon the Ford was curving up through the cloverleaf toward downtown Des Moines. The city seemed immense to Roxanne, immense and unwelcoming. She tried to fire herself up with excitement for the adventure, but it didn't work.

They stopped for hamburgers, and bought a Sunday paper that gave them addresses of several places offering rooms for rent. The first they visited was for men only, but the second specialized in working girls, and it appealed to both Roxanne and Thora. It was a large old home just north of Grand Avenue, close to downtown and the bus lines. It was a boxy frame building painted a mustard color, with porches jutting out on all three stories.

Thora did most of the talking, and Roxanne was content to let her. It was suddenly a precious luxury, having a mother to take care of her.

The room that the landlady showed them was small but pleasant, with a maple bed and shaggy carpet and a glassed-in porch. It was at the top of the house with a view of the backyard and the backs of other houses, and the little bit of green grass made Roxanne ache for her farm. But in general she was happy with the room, and glad to have the first hurdle over with. Now it would just be a matter of finding a job before her five hundred dollars ran out.

When Roxanne's new landlady finally left them alone, she stood facing her mother, awkward now that the time was here.

She tried to think of something to say.

"Thanks for bringing me down, Mom."

Thora said, "First thing you do, you find a bank and open a checking account, so you don't lose that money. Okay?"

Roxanne nodded.

"You don't have to stay here, you know, not if you're not going to be happy. That farm is as much yours as it is mine. It's your home, any time you want it to be."

"I know that. Thanks."

There was so much more that needed to be said, that Roxanne's mind froze. She saw her mother hold out her arms, and Roxanne went in to that comfort.

"You'll be coming home Christmas?"

"Yes. I will. I'll be home Christmas. And Mom?"

"What?"

"I don't know. Thanks, I guess."

"You be happy, now, hear?" Thora's voice was suddenly rough. "You figure out what you want out of your life, and don't you settle for less."

Thora turned her big head away and moved quickly down the hall, down the stairs, and out of the house.

SIX

It was just six, but already full dark, when Thora turned at the mailbox and bumped slowly up her lane. The yard light had turned itself on at dusk, and it illuminated the parking place where the pickup truck was not.

This is it, she thought as she parked the Ford and got out. No, maybe not. He might just be in town or over at his dad's or someplace.

She turned away from the house and went to the barn instead. Once inside the house she'd know for sure, and suddenly she was in no hurry to know. One look over the fence at the impatient, accusing cattle told her that the evening chores were still to be done. With a sense of relief for the welcome routine, Thora jammed up the handle on the water pump in the yearlings' lot and went inside the barn, up the steep ladder stairs to the loft, aware of her town slacks and shoes but not much caring.

In the huge vaulted loft she stopped and stood and felt diminished by the towers of hay bales that reached above her, three times her height. What a monument to their labor, she thought, hers and

101

Clete's and Roxanne's, all those long, hot, sweaty, itchy days in May and July and September, all those days of mowing and conditioning and baling and loading and hauling, and elevating the fragrant green bales up into the loft, Thora below on the hay wagon feeding bales onto the elevator and Clete and Roxanne up here receiving the bales and stacking them in stairstep mountains.

Thora hadn't been in the loft for months, hadn't done chores since last winter, couldn't remember how many bales went to each lot.

Roxanne always took care of it, she thought, aching. I'll just have to take a guess.

She threw several down for the yearlings—no horse in with them now—and several more for the bull and stock cows, and another several to be carried to—no. She looked down from the north door and the weanling calves were standing directly below, looking up, waiting for supper to come thumping down on them.

No more carrying to the weanlings. Roxanne's Saturday labor stood visible down there, stout wooden fence posts perfectly aligned and strung with taut barbed wire. Had Roxy known who was going to be doing the chores, Thora wondered, bemused. Would she have gone to all that work to make things easier for her father? No, not likely.

Would she, for me?

She did, didn't she?

If Thora Armstrong were an easy-crying woman she would have cried then instead of just leaning her braided head against the splintery door frame, cried not for the loss of her husband and marriage, not even for the leaving of her daughter, but for this wood and wire evidence that there was indeed one human being who loved her.

For the first time since her puppyhood bout with distemper Boots was invited into the house that evening. She was overwhelmingly grateful and lay beneath the kitchen table all through Thora's supper, thumping her tail against the floor and wriggling against Thora's feet.

Thora ate, as Roxanne ate, because it was mealtime and the engine needed fuel. Clete's note lay on the table, half propped against the sugar bowl, one corner made transparent by its contact with the butter dish. She had read it, then left it where it lay while she went about knocking the cat off the counter and warming leftovers of meatloaf and green beans. It was what she'd expected, the note, no explanations, just the information that he was going back to Waterloo and the Deere plant, would let her know when he had an address, would either go along with a divorce if she wanted one or just let things go as they were.

Not that explanations were necessary. Thora tried to remember just when she had begun to know that Clete was biding his time until Roxanne left home, that he was planning his own escape. She couldn't pinpoint it, it was just something she had known, and accepted, and welcomed.

She washed her few supper dishes, and the breakfast things, then with Boots close at her feet she went upstairs. The middle-sized suitcase was gone. She nodded. His rifles were gone from the spare bedroom, and also the heavy patchwork quilt that should have been folded atop the cedar chest. Why did he take that, she wondered. But it didn't matter.

She stood in the door of Roxanne's room and looked around, aching at its neatness. Something was missing here, too. Her eyes went over every detail of the room, remembering what Roxanne had packed and what she had left. There had been two snapshots stuck in the mirror frame that were not there now, snapshots of Roxanne on Buck.

Down in her own bedroom Thora checked the big maple wardrobe that had been Clete's. All his farm clothes were still there. I'll pack them up tomorrow, and store them away, she decided.

She sat in the living room in her television chair, but left the room dark and silent. It seemed to be the time to reflect back upon her marriage, analyze it, mourn for it. But she couldn't seem to keep her mind on it. Clete was gone. That was all. Although there were uneasy rufflings on the surface of her thoughts—Clete's dad was going to give him hell for leaving his family; there would be the divorce to decide about; neighbors to tell—the deeper part of her mind was at peace. For the first time in thirty years Thora Braun felt that she belonged to herself.

Light came softly into the room from the yard light outside the windows, from the flame in the oil stove beside Thora's chair, just enough light to outline the shape of her, sunk deep in her recliner. She looked down the length of herself in her stretched-out old sweater and her old checked wool slacks, and she thought, here sits the queen of the farm. She smiled at the thought.

After a while the practicalities of the situation pressed down upon her. I can't do it alone, she told herself. Clete won't be that much of a loss, but Roxanne—If only Roxanne's choice had been the farm. The two of them could do it. The two of them—Thora smiled again, then the smile fell away. No, Roxanne had her own needs, and they apparently lay elsewhere.

I could tell her. I could call her and tell her her father has left. No. Roxanne would come. She'd come because she'd know I need her help with the farm. No, I won't say anything. She'll be here at Christmas, and she'll see the situation, but I won't ask her to come back.

But oh, Lord, how I hope—

SEVEN

The Metro Life building occupied half a city block in downtown Des Moines, and its claims department filled the entire twelfth floor, so Roxanne's territory was vast, although it was cluttered with clots of desks half-partitioned from neighboring clots of desks by barriers of file cabinets.

Roxanne had her own desk, a small wooden one barely more than a work table in a double row with five other file clerks' desks near a huge bank of files, but it was her own and she felt almost tender toward it. It was her home in this vast complicated world. Along two sides of the twelfth floor were the claims adjusters' offices, small gray metal cubicles that Roxanne found more depressing than the openness out here in the middle. The other two walls were mostly windows. Through the windows nearest her desk Roxanne could see the gilded dome of the state capitol building several blocks east across the river. It gave her a nice feeling when she thought about it, which wasn't often. Today the sky beyond the windows was a high light blue, and shafts of pale March sun lightened the desk tops along the west wall.

It was almost four-thirty. Already most of the secretaries had covered their typewriters and were standing around each other's desks comparing plans for the weekend. All but the most diligent of the adjusters were gone from their offices, and all but two of Roxanne's fellow file clerks had already done their Friday afternoon fade-away.

Roxanne sat hunched over the typewriter she shared with the other file clerks. It was an old manual on a rolling steel stand, hardly related to the sleek humming IBMs on the secretaries' desks, but Roxanne liked it. It was more controllable than the electrics. She was typing a long roll of labels for file folders, easy work, like most of her job; the adjusters gave her lists of new cases and she made up files for them, with carefully typed labels, metal clasps, and the basic forms for opening a new claims case.

After three and a half months in this office, Roxanne was beginning to relax and enjoy it. Most of the fifteen floors of Metro Life were still a mystery to her, but she knew her way around the places she needed to know, and she was intimately familiar with the bank of central files, which was her primary responsibility. She no longer came to the office every morning with a clenched stomach, dreading to make a mistake or to be given a job she didn't understand. In fact the work was pleasantly confined. All there'd been for her to learn was the filing system, which was orderly and logical. After that it was a matter of caring for it, of eating away at the baskets of things to be filed away, of pulling files requested by secretaries and adjusters and, when there was nothing else to do, of going through the files to be sure all the folders were in their proper places.

It pleased Roxanne to know she had mastered her job. That it was one of the lowest jobs in the company did not disturb her; it was to be expected. She had been even more pleased, after a month or so on the job, to begin to realize that she was one of the better file clerks in the department. Most of the other girls were dull-minded and easily confused or else just flat-out silly, in Roxanne's opinion. They gave minimal attention to their work and put nearly all their energy into watching the men and gossiping.

The stillness of the room finally caught Roxanne's attention. She looked up to see an empty room, covered typewriters. Carefully she pulled the roll of labels out of the typewriter and stored it in her desk drawer, covered her typewriter, and got her purse and jacket. But at the elevator she went up instead of down.

The fifteenth floor was Roxanne's favorite. Here were badminton and handball courts, two bowling lanes and a volleyball court, ping pong table, pool table, and the card tables. In-office recreation, it was called, provided for the physical and mental benefit of Metro Life's employees, and also to keep Metro Life's teams competitive in inter-city league competition. Although the fifteenth floor wasn't big enough for a basketball court, the company did have a team which ranked high in the city's Women's League. The unusually high interest in girls' high school basketball in Iowa's small towns created a fine spawning ground for talent, and large numbers of these rural girls came, as Roxanne had, to the large insurance companies in Des Moines, where the pay scale was too low to attract the sophisticated but where employment was easy to get. Roxanne had tried out for the basketball team and hadn't made it, but that was all right. It wouldn't have been the same without Norma, she reasoned.

Often after work she came up to fifteen for an informal volleyball game with whomever felt like playing, usually other clerks, a few secretaries, occasionally a young man or two from the sales trainee program. Social strata were well defined on the fifteenth floor. Top-level executives got the handball court, younger executives and higher-up secretaries played badminton, salesmen bowled and played pool. Volleyball was the realm of the young, unskilled office girls. The secretaries seldom played. They appeared to have better things to do with their time.

Today the volleyball court was empty. In fact, most of fifteen was empty. Friday afternoon, of course, Roxanne thought. Nobody wants to hang around the office on Friday. Well, that's all right, she thought, smiling. I've got a date myself, no need for me to be killing time up here. I've got a date.

Not all that much of a date, she thought, riding down to street level in the elevator. Randy was getting tiresome. Six dates, no, seven, and already she was only going out with him because it felt so good to have dates after all those years in high school without them.

Randy was a big soft young man who always seemed to be coming untucked or unzipped around the middle. No matter what he wore there was always a triangle of undershirt showing just above his belt buckle, and his suits always seemed to be flecked with loose hair, dandruff, lint. He was nice enough. He had big warm eyes behind his heavy glasses, and he'd developed a sort of puppyish adoration of Roxanne, which she relished. But she could no longer avoid the realization that Randy just wasn't what she wanted.

He was inordinately proud of his civil service job at the post office, and he was obviously looking for a wife. I could have him, Roxanne told herself. I could probably get him to propose tonight, and then I'd have a diamond on my left hand, and a bridal shower, and a wedding in the chapel at First Methodist, and then a little house out in some subdivision, and babies.

This dismal chain of possibilities carried her out of the building and onto her bus, and most of the way home. She walked up the hill from the bus stop to the big mustard-colored house thinking how nice it was to have a chance at those things, and to choose not to choose them.

She unzipped her jacket and threw her head back. Even here with the air full of exhaust fumes she could still find the wet green smell of spring. Already spring. In another two weeks the work would be starting on the farm. Her period of indecision was going to have to end. Now.

"Afternoon, Roxy," her landlady called from the side yard where she was examining the lilacs for buds. Roxanne lifted her hand from her jacket pocket and returned the greeting.

Inside, on the stairway, she had a near collision with Beth and Jeannie, who shared a room on the second floor. They were young and slim and chattery, not especially pretty girls, but outgoing and kind. They worked at the telephone company. It was at their insistence that Roxanne had gone to a Christmas party given by the young adult group from their church, and had met Randy and the others who now made up Roxanne's circle of friends. Most were young men and women from rural areas who worked in Des Moines and lived in respectable rooming houses or inexpensive apartments, who were not comfortable in the singles bars and country clubs; who alleviated their loneliness and need for romance at Thursday night meetings of Young Adult Fellowship, and at the low-keyed parties and picnics that were spin-offs from the group.

"Roxie. There you are, we were just looking for you," Jeannie said breathlessly. "Come on, go with us. We're going up to Noah's Ark for pizza, and maybe go to a show or something after. Want to come?"

"I can't. I've got a date with Randy." She was genuinely sorry. Jeannie and Beth would have been livelier company.

They followed her up to her room, and made themselves comfortable on her bed while she opened the windows of her little porch and smelled the spring.

"Is it getting serious with Randy?" Beth asked.

"Nope." Roxanne sat down heavily in her one chair and kicked off her shoes. "Well, he's serious, but I'm not."

"Good," Beth said, bouncing, "because we've just decided we're going to get an apartment, and we want you to come in on it with us. Will you? You got your three-month raise, and Jeannie's a supervisor now, so we should all be able to afford it. Actually, our rent shouldn't be any more than we're paying here, and just think how much more fun it will be to have our own place, where we can entertain our dates, and cook our meals instead of eating out all the time."

"That alone will save us a bunch of money," Jeannie said.

Roxanne looked at the two of them and thought how much fun it might be to share an apartment with them. An apartment was the next step up, of that she was sure. But—

She said, "There's something I have to think about. I can't talk about it yet, I have to think about it some more, but if I stay in Des Moines, then I'd love to go in with you on the apartment. It's nice of you to want me to. I'll make up my mind by tomorrow, okay?"

They left and Roxanne went out onto her porch to stand with her forehead against the cool glass. In the yard below, patches of dirty snow lay melting under the lilacs. She thought, at home the snow is deeper. And cleaner. And the cows will be far enough along so you can tell which ones are going to calf by the shape of their sides, looking from behind. It'll be time to sell the yearlings. How is Mom going to manage that? She'll never be able to get them loaded through that loading chute by herself. And she won't want to ask the neighbors to help, not when they're all so busy with their own work. And she'll have to be getting the cropland rented out if I'm not—if she won't be able to farm it herself. I have to decide.

She remembered how it was at Christmas, going home and finding her mother alone, deserted. Coping. Coping cheerfully, to Roxanne's surprise. Somehow she was not surprised at her father's leaving. He had never belonged to the farm, she knew. Not the way Thora did. Not the way she did, herself. His absence was upsetting only at first. Then it began to seem as though he were a distant relative, living in his proper place in Waterloo.

Roxanne smiled now, realizing that it was the best Christmas she could remember. Her mother had apparently spent the entire month of December preparing for it. There were boxes and boxes of mother-sewn clothes for Roxanne, suitable for office work and city dates. The house was decorated on every available surface with things Roxanne hadn't seen in years, the crèche she herself had made in fourth grade, and candles and foil garlands and the old, old red felt Christmas table cloth. Everything but the tree. And as soon as Roxanne had time to change into her dear comfortable farm clothes she and Thora kicked the old Case tractor into life and rode far out into the pasture to cut a small spruce and haul it home. Inside the living room the tree that had looked small outdoors took on size and stature, and entirely filled the corner between the television and the closet door. Such an old-fashioned thing to do, they told each other, going out on your own land and cutting a Christmas tree on Christmas eve afternoon; they had always bought their trees three weeks ahead of time at the grocery store before. But they smiled at each other about it, and felt warmed.

They had talked, then, about the future. Thora's tone had been assuring, and yet somehow open-ended, as though leaving room for options, as she told Roxanne the farm would be no problem. She could do the livestock chores herself, everything except the crops. The cornfields could be rented to neighbors, and the hay could be harvested on shares with someone in the area. Not as much money coming in as there would be if they were working the land themselves, but enough for Thora to live on.

Roxanne said little, but thought heavily during those three days of Christmas vacation. She wanted to say, Mother, I'll come home and you and I will work the farm together. She wanted that so much, so very much. But that was in December, when she was still feeling new and intimidated at Metro Life, still finding her way with the buses and feeling stiff-faced with the girls in the other rooms at the boarding house. When she tried to sort out her feelings about the farm, and Des Moines, it was impossible to tell whether she wanted to come home because it was the right place for her to spend her life, or because it would be so much easier than going on with things in Des Moines.

She closed her eyes and strained to see straight through her muddled thoughts, to the core of the problem. How do I feel now? Is it any different now?

Yes. Yes, it is. I got my three-month raise, and my supervisor's evaluation said I was a fine, dependable worker with a better than average sense of responsibility. I got a job and I learned it, and I was good at it. I made friends. I got a boyfriend, and I learned how to get around town on the buses. I did it. I was scared to death to come here, but I came anyway and proved I could do it. Now the question is, is this where I really belong?

She thought of the intensity in her mother's voice when Thora told her to find out what she really wanted, and not to settle for less. And Roxanne began to understand. Marrying Randy, or someone like him, would be settling for less than the life that, from the deepest part of her, Roxanne knew to be the only existence she was meant for.

When she turned away from the window her face was older, calmer, stronger. She looked very much like Thora.

A late spring storm blew across the farm with a mixture of rain and small, hard snowflakes. The grass was green already, and at the side of the house, tulips' red cups filled with snow. In the barn loft a coveralled figure in a dark blue stocking cap moved from hay piles to windows, throwing down bale after bale of the last of the hay supply, eight for the young calves, twelve for the bull and stock cows, eight for the soon-to-be-marketed yearlings, and for the young sorrel quarter horse who stood among them.

The coveralled figure came down the loft stairs, out of the barn, and into the chicken house, then out again and across the yard to the house, a small black border collie at her heels. On the landing, she kicked off her boots, then stepped up into the kitchen.

"Here," she said, fishing from her coverall pockets seven eggs and holding them out.

Thora received them. "The girls are doing better. That's seventeen eggs today. Must be the weather warming up, huh?"

"It's snowing a little, in with the rain," Roxanne said as she kicked her way out of the coveralls. "It's going to be a nasty night out."

They sat down to supper, comfortably smug in the knowledge that they were in for the evening and bad weather needn't bother them. The dog curled up under the table, between her two favorite pair of feet; the cat began his cautious advance toward the skillet in the sink, a wary eye on Thora. The two women ate their meal wordlessly, but with pleasure.